Ben Hewitt's *I Toss Till Dawn* draws one in as almost participant-observer in the self-discovery odyssey of the young Chase Pollard. With just the right disjointed feel of impulsive courage endeavoring on the pinball realm of an open-ended road trip, Hewitt has one trying to help Chase find continuity and meaning in the successive challenges of his journey. Yet he eschews the easy answer or the facile and predictable resolution for which other writers might settle. Reality has a history and a future, yet to live as fully as possible in the serendipitous unfolding of each moment brings an awareness tantamount to revelation, and Hewitt's Chase Pollard doggedly seeks just such an epiphany.

—D. Richmond, professor of philosophy,
Grand Canyon University

Ben Hewitt rejuvenates Kerouac's road trip with this earnest and provocative Gen Y adventure. Settle in for a compelling read.

—Mary Clyde, author of *Survival Rates*

I
TOSS
TILL
DAWN

BEN HEWITT

I
TOSS
TILL
DAWN

TATE PUBLISHING & Enterprises

Published by Tate Publishing & Enterprises, LLC
127 E. Trade Center Terrace | Mustang, Oklahoma 73064 USA
1.888.361.9473 | www.tatepublishing.com

Tate Publishing is committed to excellence in the publishing industry. The company reflects the philosophy established by the founders, based on Psalm 68:11,
"The Lord gave the word and great was the company of those who published it."

Book design copyright © 2010 by Tate Publishing, LLC. All rights reserved.
Cover design by Tyler Evans
Interior design by Lindsay B. Behrens

Published in the United States of America

ISBN: 978-1-61663-056-0
1. Fiction / General   2. Fiction / Coming Of Age
10.03.03

For Jeff and Alex

Kathleen,
Thanks so much for
your support and Friendship
over the years! I've
always enjoyed having you
and your Family in my
life. I hope you
enjoy the book.
~ Ben Hewitt

ACKNOWLEDGEMENTS

A very special thanks to
Bari Mitchell, Patti Yeager, Janet Lindquist,
Emily Wilson, Melissa Huffer,
and everyone else who played
a part in helping this book come
to print. I am forever grateful
to each and every one of you.

Who is the third who walks always beside you?
—T.S. Eliot, *The Waste Land*

So I have been allotted months of futility, and nights of misery have been assigned to me. When I lie down I think, "How long before I get up?" The night drags on, and I toss till dawn.
—Job 7:3–4 (NIV)

AWAKENING

*Journal
June 21, 2009*

If you value your time you should stop reading now. There is nothing of worth in anything I have to say. I sit alone on top of this parking garage staring out across the lights and shapes...

Chase Pollard was tired, but no matter how hard he tried, he could not go back to sleep. He rolled over in his bed and buried his head under his pillow. His eyes burned with exhaustion, but his mind wouldn't be quiet. Frustrated, he sat up in bed. There was nothing he could think of that was worth getting up for.

Everything he knew was not enough. His world was wrong.

Across the room from where he sat, a small mirror hung on the wall. In the half-light of the morning, Chase stared at his reflection. The face looking back at him was thin, with light brown hair that came down over his ears. His eyes were dark blue, mirroring a thoughtful deeper nature. Lately, though, these same eyes had taken on an underlying grief—there was an inner anguish shining out from those eyes. It gave him a tired look, like one who struggles with insomnia.

Chase sat for a long time examining his reflection without moving. He didn't want to get out of bed. His gaze shifted around his room. Along one wall sat an old desk; some forgotten school work littered the surface. Hanging from the wall above this desk, his high school diploma faced him. He shook his head in wonder, mumbling to himself that in just three months he would enter college. His sight shifted lazily to his bookshelf. Works of Faulkner, Camus, and Plath, among others, sat adorning the shelves. As he had grown, he found himself more and more interested in understanding himself and the world around him. He was drawn toward art and seeking truths. This curiosity had gradually shifted to a burden. As he read, more and more doors opened before him—doors that were much easier opened than closed. He stared up at his books miserably. A sad, ironic smile crept onto his face. Speaking out loud, to only himself, he mused:

"So many books…so many questions…so many problems."

He saw no answer, nothing.

His eyes fell to the floor near his bed. There, tossed on the floor, was a tattered notebook. Its spine was nearly broken, and the pages were bent from lying upside down. Chase stared at the worn surface of his journal, and thought about the desperation he'd felt the night before, when he had sat on the top floor of an empty parking garage. Suddenly, Staring at the journal, something happened to him.

Chase felt his eyes harden. Everything weak and scared inside of him was ignored. There was a wild desire to do something, anything! He stood up, alone— knowing that he was lost—but refusing to accept it. Everything he knew was not enough, and that meant only one thing to Chase in that moment.

I can't stay here…I have to get away.

The idea was sudden and consuming. *I should leave,* he thought. *I need to just get away from everything. I can do it. I can just drive.*

Chase leapt up from his bed. The hollow resignation from moments before had been overcome with an angry desire to escape. There was an energetic madness coursing through his veins. His mind was racing.

Picking up some crumpled clothes on his floor, he hastily dressed, then walked over to the closet and grabbed his backpack. He packed the bag with several changes of clothing, grabbed his pillow and sleeping bag, and three hundred dollars in graduation money that had been sent by various friends and family. *I need a road map too,* he thought as he looked at everything in his bag. *And some food probably... I can grab both downstairs before I leave.* Pausing to double check his room for anything else that might add to his absurd quest, his eyes paused once again on his bookshelf. *Should I bring some books for company?* he wondered briefly. *No—I need to get away from all this. I need to find something new, something real.* As he grabbed his bag, he saw his cell phone sitting on his desk. He frowned. *No,* he thought, *not that. I have to get away from it all.*

Turning suddenly, he dashed from the room, nearly colliding with his younger sister, Abigail.

"Hey!" she cried irritably. "Where are you running to? It's summer, you know—you don't have school today."

"I know. Sorry, Abs," he replied, still walking.

His house was not grand, yet it was inviting. This was due largely to his mother's profession—interior design. She had an eye for color and style, and made use of it, buying random towel racks or special color-coordinated picture frames just because. She could never leave her work at work. If something caught her eye in the store, she would buy it, whether or not there was a place or a reason for it. She was never happier than when she was rearranging knickknacks and doodahs.

Chase failed to notice any of these surroundings this morning. He was completely consumed on one thought: departure. He had reached a breaking point, and something had to happen. Everything inside of him longed for some semblance of purpose or truth. School, art, friends, life—where was the point in it all? As he descended the stairs, he determined what he would do. *I will take my time, free my mind, and drive,* he thought. *I don't know where I'll go, but that really doesn't matter. Anything is better than rotting here.* These were his thoughts as he bustled along, loading only the bare essentials into his Jeep.

It was nearly noon as he hurried downstairs for the last time. He shot a quick glance over his shoulder. It was best that he go unnoticed. He resolved to call his parents from a pay phone once decidedly out of reach. He had nothing against his parents, but he had no desire to try talking to them.

His Jeep, a forest green, 1992 Cherokee, had required quite a lot of working and saving on his part. His parents had matched the money he raised, but it still had taken him a fairly long amount of time to acquire the necessary funds to purchase it. It was a reliable car, though, and he had never regretted his choice.

Sitting behind the wheel of the car, he felt a wave of uncertainty crash over him. *What am I doing? Who in their right mind wakes up and just runs away? Am I losing it?* He sat lost amid a swirl of thoughts. He started to open the door to walk back inside when, as if by some divine hand, a realization struck him:

"I know everything that's here if I stay," he thought aloud. "Out there, though ... there is no familiarity or certainty. The only way to break free from the known and redundant cycle is to run after the hope of things unknown. If I stay here, I'm accepting more of the same. Without risks, there is no chance of anything better."

Chase smiled as lines of an old Robert Frost poem crossed his mind:

> Two roads diverged in a wood, and I—
> I took the one less traveled by,
> And that has made all the difference.

Chase started the engine and backed from the garage.

RUNNING

The neighborhood rolled slowly by as he drove toward the nearest gas station. The day was overcast. Houses huddled behind their fenced-off lawns. Trees stood tall with arms outstretched to the sky—coaxing, inviting the rain. Their leaves stood out sharp in the cool afternoon breeze. Everything was gray. The clouds in the sky were dark and heavy with tears. They cast a long shadow over the early summer day. Chase felt cold and turned on the heat inside his car. The air was like stagnant, hot breath. The road wound on.

Chase pulled into a gas station not far from his neighborhood. He absentmindedly put the nozzle in his car as he walked inside.

"Yeah, I'm just filling up, he told the man behind the counter. Also I'll take two packs of Camels," he said.

"That'll be $58.50," the man behind the counter said as he rung him up.

Chase cringed on hearing the cost, but he had already known the price would be high. He handed him the cash, took his cigarettes, and walked out the door. He suddenly realized the man hadn't even asked to see his ID. This thought perturbed him, thinking that the signs of stress were weighing more heavily on his features, already aging his young body. He glanced down at the cigarettes lying next to him on the passenger seat.

It was two in the morning. Chase sat smoking with his friend Kurt near their school. Chase had many acquaintances, but few people he considered real friends. Kurt was one of those few. They had been sitting there talking for several hours. The brisk night air nipped at the skin of their exposed faces, but they didn't seem to notice.

"I just don't really know what to do with my life," Chase admitted as he inhaled deeply from his cigarette. "There is nothing that jumps out at me as worth doing."

"Yeah it's definitely a tough choice, but man, you've still got like your first year at college where you can just take general courses and not have to declare any sort of major," said Kurt.

They both sat silent, staring out across the football field from up in the stands, each wrapped in their own thoughts of what the future might hold. Finally Chase spoke.

"I'm really going to miss you next year when you're out of state for school. I feel like I've slowly been alienating myself from people here. Friends I used to have, I don't really even talk to anymore. And the sad part is I don't even care … it's like I'm becoming indifferent to them all. I have a hard time relating. It's like I'm purposely avoiding people, because I just don't feel like interacting. I mean, look at me—I'm eighteen years old, for crying out loud! But I spend a lot of time just sitting alone wondering, 'what's the point of it all?' Why the hell do I feel like that? I mean, really, what do I have to be so depressed about?"

"Hey I can somewhat relate—you know how emotional I can be at times. Honestly, I don't know why we, or people like us, feel this way. Like, we have good families, jobs, and money if we need it, and we're pretty good students. I definitely agree that it really doesn't make sense. All I can think is that things will be better once we get to college. We'll make new friends and kind of get a fresh start in a way, ya know? This is a super stressful and tough time in most people's lives, but they seem to make it. Why shouldn't we? It'll get better. You just have to give it some time."

"What if we're missing something? What if it doesn't get better as we get older? I don't understand it, but something inside me is screaming, and I don't know why. At night it's the worst. I lie in bed just thinking—sometimes for hours without sleeping. And often, when I'm alone and cut off inside my own mind, I lay there thinking 'I wish I wasn't here.'"

It was quiet then. Neither of them spoke. They were together, but miles apart. Both sat staring off into the darkness.

Chase shook the memory off, trembling at the vivid clarity of this past event. With an act of willpower, he pushed out the thoughts of despair that seemed to all but consume him. He turned the key. The car fired to life upon request, and Chase began driving down the long road ahead.

The lines on the pavement streaked by. The radio played softly as he rolled along. He had been driving west now for about three hours and had just passed from Illinois into Iowa. The drive so far had had a calming effect on him. His mind was placid and absent of any dark thoughts. He heard the music, saw the towns and roads, and felt mildly content. Soon though, he would have to call his parents, and that suppressed knowledge slowly unnerved his feeling of apathy.

He pulled into a restaurant for dinner. It was the first time since he had gotten gas that he had stopped for anything. He moaned as he stretched out his body and legs and walked stiffly toward the door. Once inside, he was escorted to a table and left to ponder the menu. He was surprisingly hungry for someone having done nothing but sit for several hours, and proceeded to dictate his order.

"Hi, yeah, I'd like the barbeque bacon burger, no tomatoes, a salad instead of soup, a large Sprite, and if I could get an appetizer of onion rings that would be great."

His waitress smiled knowingly, commenting on the tremendous appetite of teenaged boys as she walked off. The room where he sat was dimly lit with an orange aura that resonated all through the place. He gazed slowly about the room taking everything in. There weren't many other people there, which being dinner hour, made him question the quality of the food. This fear was put to rest after he bit into his appetizer. He was pleasantly surprised, and as he worked through his meal, he started trying to formulate what he would say to his parents.

So, Dad, Mom—he thought as he ate—*how are you? Oh, well, that's good. Are you sitting down? Great, 'cause I'm in Iowa, traveling West with no real destination in mind, with a pillow, sleeping bag, and $242.50—not factoring in what I just spent on food. So yeah ... later!*

Chase let out a short laugh as he pictured the looks on their faces. Seeing how that route would no doubt lead to a load of unnecessary trouble, he opted for something more in the gray area of honesty. The remainder of his dinner was spent shuffling through different explanations he could give to his parents. Finally, after finishing his dinner and leaving a generous tip, he set his sights on the pay phone across the room and walked over.

Reaching the phone, Chase paused for one last minute to gather his nerve. He had no idea how his parents would take his sudden absence. Would they empathize with his plight? Or more likely, would they hire private investigators to find and deliver him home, only to have him locked in his room until college rolled around? He shook these thoughts out of his mind, inhaled, and dialed the number. It rang three times before being picked up.

"Hello?" his mother answered.

"Hey, Mom. It's Chase."

"Oh, are you calling to let us know what your plans are for the night?"

"Yeah, something like that," he replied with a short, anxious laugh.

"Well?" she asked somewhat more alert.

Chase paused. All his practicing and planning on what to say abandoned him. He was immediately regretting making this call, and the thought of just hanging up ran through his head.

"Chase, is everything all right?" There was tension in her voice.

"Mom … I'm not going to be home for awhile," he said slowly.

"And where is it that you plan on being?" she asked.

"I'm traveling," he said weakly. "I'm just taking some time away for myself, expanding my horizons you could say. Anyway, all I'm trying to say is I've made up my mind, and I'll be home when it's all over."

He was met with silence—silence that seemed interminable. It was only for a few seconds, but it was agonizingly long for him.

Finally she said, "Your father's here. He wants to talk to you."

Chase felt his spirits plummet. His palms began to sweat—liquid anxiety oozing from his pores. How would his father take the news? Would he order him home immediately, not even pausing to listen? He and his dad had an uneasy peace at home. It was the strange sort of mutual understanding between a father and his coming-of-age son. The son pressing the set limits, and the father—needed less and less by the son—attempting to assert rigid rules, enforcing them often to just be remembered. The relationship between Chase and his father was changing. The shift was often a bitter and odious affair. Luckily, at worst there were usually only fleeting moments of animosity between them. Chase closed his eyes as his father's voice stridently sounded over the line.

"Chase?"

"Yeah, Dad."

"What's the matter, son? Is everything all right?" His voice was filled with concern.

"Everything's all right, Dad. I just need some time to myself, away from everything and everyone. I can't explain it all...but I need this, Dad." These last words were spoken in desperation.

His father was quiet for a moment, seeming to examine the weight of his son's words. Chase sat with the phone held to his ear. A heavy air hung about him. Then, after the prolonged hesitation, his father spoke.

"All right...I understand. Do what you have to do. And son...we love you. Please call if you get the chance—it'll help keep your mother's mind at ease."

"I'll do what I can," he whispered, knowing that he was lying. "Good-bye, Dad."

"Take care. Be safe."

Chase hung up the phone, feeling a sense of awe come over him. This last act brought with it a sense of finality. His self-exile was complete. There was nothing now except him. He sat still imagining what towns and countryside might lay ahead, picturing the faces of people he had never met, contemplating the sun rising up in brilliant splendor over mountains he had yet to witness, imagining star-filled skies flaming far above, and seeing always the road ever stretching itself before him.

He smiled sardonically. It was out there somewhere. He knew it but he didn't know how. The hope of release and understanding filled his mind.

Chase stood slowly and walked out the door.

JACK

Chase left the small town of Cedar Falls heading nowhere in particular. Night was beginning to come on, and he began to look for an out of the way place to stay the night. The land was flat with few trees. He drove along the small highway leading west. The road stretched steadily on, with few places to get off. After about an hour's drive, he decided to take his chances off the main road. Taking the next opportunity that presented itself, he headed off along a smaller street that seemed to lead nowhere near civilization.

He hummed softly along with the radio, staring ahead in relaxed stupor. Thoughts and images floated through his mind—none of them latching onto his thinking for very long.

A sudden jolt from a sizeable rock dissipated any further daydreaming. Chase looked around, scanning his surroundings. This new road was less sure than the one he had left. It continued to wind on for several miles before coming to a split. One way led to a small town. Standing next to the other street was a sign that simply read "Dead End." Hoping to find a deserted area to camp the night out, he went down the dead-end street. He had no real plan. He simply thought that as long as there weren't many people around, it didn't really matter much where he slept.

The street was old and crude, worse even than the former. Chase drove slowly in order to avoid various potholes. His Jeep lumbered along. The gentle bumping of the street on his car had a sleep inducing effect on him. He felt his eyelids begin to droop, and his muscles slacken. He doggedly shook the sleep away, though only momentarily, and took to rubbing his eyes frequently.

"Come on, Chase," he said to himself, "sleep *after* we stop driving."

Several houses sat staring blankly toward him as he passed by. *Farming land, mostly,* he thought. Then the road curved slowly left and arrived finally at its destination. There was a sort of cul-de-sac area in which to turn around, and a barred gate leading out into a pasture. There were no houses around, just the gate leading into an open field and the road he had been driving on. Two trees sat drooping near the gates entrance. Apart from that, however, it was much like the rest of the countryside. He stopped the car and got out.

He was getting jittery and anxious. It had been a full day without a cigarette. He was able to hold off smoking for a day, or two at best, but the nicotine always helped. He pulled out his Zippo lighter, and lit up his first one of the night. The drug instantly began to calm his nerves. Sitting on top of his Jeep, he inhaled deeply—holding it in, relishing the effect. His parents didn't know anything about this habit. *It wouldn't really matter if they did know though*, he thought, *I'm old enough now to smoke legally.* When he had first started smoking at fourteen, he had to have other people buy for him.

At first, it was just to try it out. It even caused him to get sick the first time, but he was persistent. It soon developed into a small habit. The routine was one smoke before school, one or two at lunch, another one or two afterwards with a buddy, and occasionally one before bed. He understood everything filthy and harmful about it. *Who in this generation doesn't*, he thought. Still he was uncaring, and willfully apathetic to the bad. He had an understanding of the bad. He chose to partake regardless. In the far recesses of his mind, he told himself that one day he would kick the habit. There were no consequences and no reason to stop yet, so it could wait a while longer.

The night was clear and warm. The earth, heated all day by the sun's rays, cooled slowly as the sun sank beyond the horizon. Chase marveled silently at the starry host above. His mind flashed to Van Gough's shimmering, enflamed masterpiece. He realized that not even that could compare to nature's own startling portrait. He sat gaping at the vastness. The night sky went on forever. What was he in comparison? This thought was immediately humbling and filled with despair. He shivered, lighting another cigarette. It was right there, staring down and mocking him. Chase grimaced, grinding his teeth—he was not ready to submit to chaos. Somewhere out there beyond his current experiences, and beyond everything the world tried to convince him of, was something. At least, he hoped there was. Chase flicked his cigarette butt away disdainfully and took to pacing in front of his car, muttering aloud like one teetering on the brink of sanity. "Suppose they're right, and this is it. What then?" he mumbled to himself.

"Well what's wrong with that? Lot's of people just go along through life caring only about their few needs, quite content and without many cares. They seem to cope just fine without needing anything more," he answered quite unconvinced.

"Yes, but are they really? Or do they simply not know where to look or who to ask? Or does it even matter which is which if nothing matters? Hell, to be ignorant would be a blessing in a situation like this," he countered, spinning quickly.

"Yet, the existentialist would say that once one has accepted the inevitability of their pointless existence, they can then find peace in the whole thing—as much peace as that leaves."

Chase was completely caught up in this heated discussion with himself. The immense turmoil in his soul was bubbling out with ludicrous zeal. He continued the debate, walking quickly back and forth.

"All right, but existentialism is only one branch of philosophy or idea, what of other philosophers and ideas over the ages? What of Plato, Confucius, Nietzsche, or Thoreau? They are all significantly different—but they all hold man in higher regard than any form of nihilism. They all see some kind of human moral, or maybe moral is slightly too strong a word, but they all see humanity as being endowed by some kind of higher function. They see admirable qualities as something *worth* striving for. In a strict existential mindset, there is no right or wrong, no good or evil. How could there be? Their whole theory is propagated on the assumption that this is it, nothing beyond what we can see or know by our own intelligence is real … and even that may be false. So now what? Where does that leave humanity?

"Although, should good and evil, right and wrong not exist at all, why do we have any sort of understanding of them?" Chase paused for a moment in contemplation. "Unless," he continued, "they are human institutions brought on by some sort of Darwinian device for the betterment and safety of our species..."

"Yes, but wouldn't that just be some sort of cautionary means of thought?" He combated. "Humans seem to have a complex system of ethics... even those that would not be beneficiary to the survival of oneself."

He stopped, thinking of honor on the battlefield, of courage to lay down one's life for another when there was absolutely no reason to. Somehow the basic instinct to live was being suppressed by a greater one. In a strictly Darwinian sense, how could this be?

"Does this support antithesis then? Is there such a thing as right and wrong? Well, morals seem to be set by humans to effectively govern themselves and live peacefully, which leaves nothing more than a development of the primordial soup that makes up our brains. Hope rests in mankind's ability to evolve past our flaws?"

Chase threw up his hands in disgust. He realized he had simply been running in circles. "If there is truth out there, then why has no one found it? Or if they have, why has the word not gotten out?" He smoldered angrily, perplexed by his own circumscribed thoughts and melancholic emotions. "If the answer is out there," he wondered quietly, "I sure don't know it." He shook his head in resignation for the night. It was still warm out. He decided to sleep under the stars, no tent, just a sleeping bag.

Chase spread his sleeping bag on the hard ground. He stretched out, wrapping himself between the inviting folds. Chase lay on his side staring out across the ground. Small tufts of light green strands were flowing upwards from the earth. They were sparse, shaggy, and patchily strewn about the ground. They were beginning to turn a golden brown. Starting from the top and stretching further and further down; aging gradually was seeping in. Expertly the summer heat had begun sucking the vitality out of their once excited strands. The life was drying out; the sublimity of youth fading more and more. In some the transformation was already complete—leaving only corpses, queerly standing at their post.

He closed his eyes, but didn't sleep. The surrounding area was silent, except for the soft whispering of crickets in the distance. He tossed back and forth, waiting for sleep's warm embrace. Laying there in the dark, being all alone became frighteningly apparent. At night feelings of hopelessness, fear, solitude, and evil became at once more alive. Their wraithlike embodiments seemed to materialize from the mystery and the stillness, each wearing its own face—taunting, mocking, and latching onto the mind. And darkness was their host. For even the most familiar surroundings, when shrouded with night's cloak, can become something more to the human imagination. To be alone was to be cut off.

Chase felt this loneliness bombard his senses. He lay curled up on the hard ground. For the first time since he had left, he was struck by intense feelings of doubt. He longed for the comfort of his own bed, for the safety and security of the familiar. These feelings welled up suddenly and strongly within his body. He tried to shove them out of his consciousness, but with little success. Thoughts of home continued to crowd his mind.

Their faces were all around him. They smiled and laughed. His mother leaned over and kissed him lightly on the forehead.

"Here it is, champ."

His father beckoned him into the garage, where a brand new bike stood glimmering in the faint light. Chase cried out, bounding toward his prize. His parents were pleased. He loved this bike unfailingly—at first.

It was barely noticeable, but after a few weeks the signs appeared more. Chase neglected the bike more often, and was not interested in it as he had been. Eventually, as with all new things, it became something he had, not something he had just gotten. It was cared for less and less. He didn't even notice its absence for some time when his parents gave it away.

Chase saw only his family, smiling back at him. He cursed his own stupidity. What had he been thinking to just up and leave? All his thoughts centered on returning home. Sitting up, he tried to regain control of his reasoning. His fingers shook he pulled from his pocket a cigarette, and after two nervous attempts he succeeded in lighting it. Tears of frustration welled up behind his eyes. He saw himself going nowhere. His naïve ambition was complete folly. With this realization came another: to turn back now would be to accept complete failure. Even in a weakened state of mind, he still acknowledged that as being the worst choice. He wiped away the hint of a tear from his eye. The momentary turmoil had dispelled, leaving in its wake a raw exhaustion. Chase fell back upon the ground, taking full advantage of this respite, and soon fell into an uneasy stupor—twisting and writhing fretfully as he lay.

Tiny clumps of water droplets sparkled in the morning light. They huddled together, galvanized by the days first rays. Their succulent, orb-like bodies joyously welcomed the sun back from its slumber.

The morning dew coldly blanketed Chase and his sleeping bag. Chase had begun to shiver under his wrappings. He tried dumbly to draw the covers tighter over his still sleeping body. The cold, mixed with morning's first sunbeams flitting over his eyelids, refused to be ignored. They roused Chase from sleep's embrace. He sat up groggily, trying to take stock of his situation.

Where am I? he thought. *And why am I outside?* Chase realized he was freezing. He leapt out of his sleeping bag and into his Jeep. There he sat, trying to both change into warmer clothes and to shake the sleepiness from his senses, having very little luck in both areas. Finally, after struggling for several minutes, he was somewhat alert and ready to be off.

The trip back to the interstate took less time than it had coming in. He drove on indifferently. The morning was dawning bright and warm, much like the day before. Chase longed for a cup of coffee, feeling like a dead man behind the wheel. He kept a weathered eye out for any place to stop. After a short drive, his diligence was rewarded as he pulled off the highway on an exit leading to an Arco gas station and a shabby diner. It was a truck stop mainly, but he saw one other car in the lot as he parked. Walking into the rundown establishment, he noted distastefully the lack of cleanliness about the place. The cushioning on the stools was ripped in many places, revealing their dirty, yellowing foam interiors. Two small windows let in rays of sunlight, but they were grimy and neglected by whatever staff worked the place. A mellow, yet distinct odor lay about the interior. It was the smell of food smothered in grease, mixed with an overall musty aroma that left Chase feeling vaguely repulsed.

He sat himself near the end of the long counter. A waitress came over holding a pot of coffee, staring grimly. She looked close to fifty, with long strands of gray weaving amongst her light brown hair. Wrinkles were beginning to set in, creasing her tanned skin. Dark, sunken eyes stared out almost in challenge. Her lips were thin and firm, and when she walked she did it with the expeditious efficiency of one whose line of work dictates such movement. "What would you like?" she asked tersely.

"I'm sorry, what?" Chase asked, snapping into the moment.

"What can I get for you?" she said again, slightly cross.

"Just some coffee," he said. "Uh, actually could I also get a bowl of Cheerios as well?"

She nodded without a word, poured him some coffee, and walked off behind the counter. Chase felt a bit foolish. His eyes pointed down at the countertop as he waited. She was back soon with his cereal, and after laying his bill on the counter, she was off once more. He took a sip of the black liquid, grimacing as the bitter fluid ran hotly down his throat. There were some sugar packets nearby. Reaching out he grabbed three, hoping to chase the bitterness from his drink. The coffee was still strong, but at least now it was bearable.

He munched slowly through his bowl of cereal, congratulating himself silently on not choosing a mound of grease for breakfast. When he finished eating, he sat back relaxing and ordered another cup of coffee.

A small television hung in the far upper corner of the room. Those customers inside who were not attending to their meals had their eyes fixed on the screen, where a news anchor droned on about an attempted bank robbery that had occurred yesterday afternoon. The newsman related how the would-be-robbers, in broad daylight, had taken hostage those inside for what seemed an "interminable" amount of time. The plot was foiled by the heroics of the Des Moines S.W.A.T. team, who, after securing the perimeter, successfully charged the bank. Two of the bandits were taken without a fight. The third shot and killed a hostage before being shot himself. The anchorman related this last part with a face wrought with forced sadness and quiet resignation. Then he promptly moved on with other news.

Chase sat still, looking out across the room. Two men near the television commented on the incident to one another.

"Fools," grunted the one nearest to Chase. "Must have been fairly desperate to plan anything like that."

"Too bad about that one person," replied his companion. "She damn sure didn't anticipate anything like that happening to her when she got up in the morning."

The other nodded morosely. They both sat silent drinking their coffee, each off in their own thoughts.

The room seemed to fade away as Chase slumped down on his stool thinking. He never knew that the victim had ever existed, and now she ceased to. That was it. The end. The man on the screen moved on without even the reflection of sorrow mirrored in his face. It was like she had never been. She was an abstraction—nothing familiar or known or certain. In some place and time she was; in this place at this time she wasn't. Was it wrong for the reporter to barely acknowledge her tragedy? Was that the only way to cope with all the misery, injustice, and death spewed across the world?

He realized it wasn't just them. He also was calloused toward much of the violence around the globe. Where was he while genocide plagued the people of Sudan? Was it not common for him to turn away from people's strife and agony, passing all feelings of guilt off by thinking there was nothing he could do? The guilt did not end with the people out there—it ended with him. He had no control over the lives of others—only his choices were in his hands. It seemed to him, as he sat there, that people only ever complained about society being the problem, not ever taking the time to realize that a society is a fusion of individuals—not a super organism that acts completely of its own accord.

Responsibility for society rests with all. Politicians can't fix the world. They are only initiators ... if that. People would have to want to change for the better and want to make the sacrifices for their fellow humans.

Here Chase paused in his chain of thought. His brow creased darkly in apprehension. He seemed to have stumbled into another wall blocking his thought process. *What though,* he wrestled slowly in his mind, *could drive a person to go beyond themselves to actually seek out what was good for another?* It bothered him that he could not find a truthful answer to this seemingly juvenile question. After struggling around the thought for a while longer, he let it slip from his mind. He arose feeling very much unsettled, paid his bill, and blundered out to the parking lot.

A cool breeze had picked up from the east, and it blew across his haggard frame. He was in no hurry, seeing as he had nowhere to be, so he lit up his first smoke of the day—protracting the calming escape without interest. He hoped to drive through Iowa today, and see how far into South Dakota he could traverse. Rubbing out his cigarette butt with the soul of his shoe, he breathed out the last of the smoke and set his eyes westward.

The road led dully on. The radio churned out the varying sound waves, reverberating throughout the car's interior, crashing continually against Chase's eardrums. He had been driving a little over an hour and had just crossed the border into South Dakota. The scenery remained faithfully unchanging. Flat patches of farmland were sown over the land. The earth, like a worn pair of jeans, was covered by the crude stitching of mankind's hand. The ground was taxed by the grinding wheels of mechanization—forced to keep up with the demands of an extravagant and wasteful society. These were the fields that rolled past, coming into his life and leaving in the same moment, leaving their indiscernible mark upon him.

Loneliness had begun to set in. The craving for another's company pressed itself upon him as he drove on. So when Chase saw a hitchhiker up ahead on the road, he veered off his course and pulled over just past the walker.

He had never picked up a hitchhiker before, and a feeling of excitement piqued inside of him. He watched in his rearview mirror as the person's shape trotted forward to meet him. The guy first opened the back door and lay his travel-sized backpack down on the seat, and then hopped into the seat opposite Chase with a grin.

"Hey, thanks a lot!" the stranger greeted affably. "I've been walking all morning out there."

"Oh yeah, no problem. I was getting pretty tired of having nothing but my own company. Where are you heading?"

"Oh I've just been traveling all over," he stated as Chase pulled out onto the road once more. "Are you heading towards Rapid City? I've got a friend out that way I'm looking to meet up with for a few days before traveling on again."

"Yeah, I think I can probably take you most of the way there, if not all the way really. I'm driving that general direction."

"Hey, that'd be great," the stranger replied, leaning back in the seat. "Saves me the hassle of having to wait around some more for another ride. I'm Jack by the way." He held out his hand in a friendly gesture.

"Chase," he replied, accepting the other's handshake.

As they made casual conversation, Chase peered out of the corner of his eye at the newcomer. He was about his own age, with shoulder length, dirty blond hair. He had a strong body, but an easygoing manner that suggested not even the slightest feelings of concern lurking under the surface. His eyes were hazel and vibrant. They radiated a full and diverse range of emotions pooled somewhere within. He laughed often as he spoke, and it was a full, inviting laugh that drew Chase in, making him feel like an essential part of the conversation. There was, as far as he could initially tell, nothing but a jovial candor about him. Chase took an active interest in what his new companion was talking about.

"So anyway," Jack was saying, "after I came home from college, I decided to hitchhike around for the summer. You can imagine my parents' response." He laughed loudly as he imitated the scene that unfolded between him and his parents.

Chase laughed along with him, feeling himself caught up in the friendliness of his travel mate. The laugh was bittersweet though. He remembered his own conversation with his parents.

"Enough about me though," Jack said. "What's your story?"

"Oh, it's nothing too exciting. I'm just on my way to see relatives in Oregon," he lied.

"Right on, I actually know a few people from over there. Whereabouts in Oregon do your relatives live?"

Chase had very little knowledge about anything in Oregon. He cursed his stupidity silently.

"Uh, come again?" he replied, trying to buy time.

"Where in Oregon are you heading?" Jack repeated.

Seeing his options narrow before his eyes, he stammered out the only place in Oregon he had ever heard of.

"Portland," Chase heard himself reply. "I'm heading to Portland."

The lie actually slid out easier than he had expected. Jack seemed to take no notice of this innocuous fib, and continued jabbering on about his experiences on the road and at college. Chase listened politely, but with less effort and concentration than before. He was paying attention, but also he was trying to size him up. What was it that made him tick? Where did this easily flowing, confident manner come from? Here was someone who seemed to have life by the tail and was enjoying the ride.

"Yeah, high school girls were always all right," Jack said, "but college chicks, man, that's where it's at!"

Chase laughed along with him, feeling like a part of his rampant escapades.

"It's really that much better then?"

"Oh, most definitely! I mean, I could always work some magic with the high school girls, but in college it's twice the action with half the work, especially at some of the parties my friends and I used to throw. You see, we didn't live on campus like a lot of the other freshmen. No, instead we had managed to get in on a house near campus where an older brother of my buddy lived. We had one of the best party houses our first year. Nice, eh?"

"No joke? That's crazy man," Chase replied.

"Yeah, it was top notch, my friend, first class all the way. But you'll see later on tonight. The guy I'm meeting up with is the same one I shared the house with this past school year. His name is Neal. He's a completely crazy guy—ha ha, I love it. He's getting together a little midsummer bash, and you, my friend, can be my guest of honor," he said, nodding approvingly.

"Thanks, man. That sounds awesome," Chase said, feeling genuine excitement run through his body.

Here it was. This was life. Chase looked up to his companion as someone far more learned and experienced in the ways of the world than he was. Perhaps just being around him for a while would help him gather a new outlook on life. In high school, he had never run with the partiers. He would make appearances at and hang out at a fair share of parties, but was never all caught up in the whole environment. With Jack it was different. This wasn't some little high school get together, no not even close—this was something bigger. This guy radiated confidence; whatever it was that made him different, Chase wanted some part.

"So what made you want to leave home for the summer and just travel around?" Chase prodded.

"Well, dude, that's not too hard to answer," he replied, grinning slyly. "Just look around you. There is so much beauty and adventure waiting out there. You might think this is like some lame overused slogan, but I believe in living everyday like it was my last. I want no part in the mainstream, work-till-you-die mindset. I think most people never take the time to enjoy life before it passes away with them slowly digging their own graves. Personally, I'd much rather just do what makes me happy—forget what other people say. It's all a matter of what works for you. I just do my own thing, and all that matters is what I feel like doing. That's why I'm out here—that's how I live."

He ended his speech, grinning widely. It was inspiring in a foolish way, his unabashed flaunting, and Chase couldn't help but secretly admire Jack's cocky audacity in the face of society's rules and regulations. His companion's self-assured nature was also a glaring reminder of his own lack of any resolution of lifestyle. And as the road wound on, and the soft murmur of the radio began fading away, a wave of despair and panic set in. He gripped the steering wheel, his knuckles beginning to turn white. Jack's voice drifted further and further away as the ever-so-familiar feeling of hopelessness came into his mind

It became more and more frequent as the year wore on. The loss of hope. The lack of caring. The insanity of not knowing. He would stay out late more and more often. And when he drove on such late nights, he drove fast.

As he drove, all of his surroundings became fake and dreamlike. He was there...but not there. He was both driving and seeing himself drive. His brain was detached from his own body. He was aware of his body acting on autopilot, while his mind floated within the bounds of his skull like a buoy in the tide. He saw the road rush beneath, saw the trees morph into a solid mass of foliage, and saw the street lamps queerly shedding their shaft of light in a dark night.

Sometimes if he went too fast around a corner, and his brakes would squeal in terror. He laughed at this. He laughed so hard sometimes that tears would begin to fall—sloppy, salty tears racing down his cheeks. His foot would automatically, as if being pulled by some hidden wire, press the gas pedal slowly downwards. His sleep-forsaken, dull mind would perceive the world both in slow motion and as an ever-expanding tunnel blossoming before him, and the corners of his mouth would lift slowly.

Someone was yelling.

"Hey, man! Slow down!"

Chase's eyes readjusted to the scene before him. He glanced down and realized that he was going just over a hundred and ten miles an hour. Jack was screaming in the seat next to him. He applied the brakes, the car slowed shakily, and then settled at a reasonable speed. Chase felt dazed, and looked toward the passenger seat.

"What the hell was that? Are you completely out of your mind?" Jack ranted.

"Sorry," Chase answered without looking over. "I guess I just kind of spaced out there for a minute."

"I would say so!" the other replied. "How's about we don't do that again, huh?"

"It won't happen again. I'm just a little bit tired I guess … not a lot of sleep last night … "

"Apparently. It looked like you were having some kind of freaking Vietnam flashback." Jack said this last part in a very caustic and sarcastic tone, but the surprised anger was leaving his voice. "We had better pull over at the next road stop and get you some coffee and have a little break."

Chase didn't argue. The incident had frightened him as much, if not more, than it had frightened Jack. How had he lost touch with reality like that? Nothing that bad had ever happened to him before during the daytime. Was he actually losing his mind? His psyche seemed to be fighting a losing battle against the insanity that threatened to overcome him. He felt like a sleepwalker in the midst of a bad dream. *Where is my escape?* he wondered, as he searched the recesses of his mind's vault, seeking some new and unexplored corner in hopes of fighting off the crushing madness kept uneasily at bay. He was tired and he was frustrated.

They pulled over at the next rest area they came upon. There were several trucks camped out in the lot and a few cars with families and groups of people. It was nearing one in the afternoon, and both Chase and Jack were feeling their hollow stomachs. There were several vending machines that they sought out, and also a table nearby with free coffee. The coffee was black and harsh, but Chase didn't care by this point. There was a fatigue that was creeping through his body. It stung his eyes and made him feel heavy. *The harsher the coffee the better,* he thought.

Taking some snacks and coffee, they trekked up a grassy hill nearby. There they sat mute and content, scarfing down their food. Jack pulled out a small bag of weed, and rolled a joint while they relaxed. They took turns hitting it, letting the calming effects lull their bodies. When they were finished, they lay out on the warm earth, feeling shoots of grass rubbing against their skin and staring up at the mellow sky. Chase let himself doze off a bit, but was soon awakened by Jack tugging at his arm.

"Rise and shine, buttercup! We gotta get goin'—now!"

Chase stumbled down the hill after him, not understanding his partner's haste. They made it to the car just as Chase heard shouting behind them. He looked back somewhat stunned. There, just where they had been resting on the hill, was a man cresting the slope who was yelling in their direction.

"What the ... ?"

"No time to explain now, ol' buddy! Get in and punch it!" Jack yelled, diving into the passenger side.

Chase followed suit, quickly turning on the engine and backing out. The man on the hill was charging down toward them. His face was crimson with rage and exertion. Fists curled menacingly; he ran after them. His eyes were fixed on Jack, and they were livid with hostility.

Chase no longer needed any encouragement from Jack; he was not about to let this mountain of man rushing down toward them tear them each in half. Adrenaline seized his body, and his hands and feet flew over the car's controls. They had just finished backing up when the man reached the parking lot. Chase floored the gas, making the Jeep lurch forward with an outraged squeal. The man was running in a collision course with the vehicle, and was racing to get in front of it to block their escape. Chase veered to the right, frantically trying to avoid the other. The enraged man was almost at the car, when by some miracle he was struck in the face with something, making him falter in his advance. They swerved past him, fleeing madly onto the freeway. Jack was leaning out the window, laughing and taunting his vanquished foe.

"What the hell was that?" Chase yelled, looking Jack square in the face.

"Whoa, easy man, easy!" he replied, still laughing. "Ya did great, kid, we're fine!"

Chase was still reeling from the shock and the adrenaline, and Jack's response did not calm him down.

"That guy looked like he was going to kill us! What in the world did you do to piss him off like that?"

"It was nothing. Just a little misunderstanding is all," Jack replied, with feigned indignation.

"No. You tell me what the hell you did to get that guy so mad."

His tone left no room for argument. Jack stared at Chase, eyes darting, and then pasted a quick, fake smile on his face.

"Well, it wasn't as bad as all that," he started innocently. "When you dozed off, I went for a walk around, and I came across this camper sitting in the far parking lot."

He paused, formulating the next fabrication in his tale. Then, deciding on his story, he continued on.

"So anyway, I noticed that their truck lights were on. I walked over there to tell somebody, but no one was around. I called out a few times, but there was no one there. So I just walked over and saw that their door was unlocked and figured it would probably be nice if I just reached in real fast and turned them off for the people.

"So I opened up the door, right?" he continued, "and I couldn't find the button anywhere. So, idiot that I am, I hopped up into the truck to try and find the switch. Ha ha. So it's about this time that I heard someone yelling from across the lot. I don't know why, but it scared me, and I took off running, and the rest you can probably fill in."

Jack finished the story, grinning. He laughed to himself as Chase rolled the story around in his mind. It seemed a bit ridiculous that they ran like mad for nothing more than a simple misunderstanding. It just didn't add up. But Jack seemed to be getting quite the kick from their mad dash, and seeing him laughing about the whole thing made him feel as if he was making a big deal out of nothing. Gradually, he joined in with his companion's laughter, and soon they were both cracking up over the incident.

"Did you see the look on his face when he was running down that hill?" Jack cried out, laughing loudly. "It was like a red balloon on steroids!"

"Or the way he was running?" Chase wheezed, joking along with him. "The guy was like a combination of Robocop and the hulk," he cried out gasping between breaths.

They heaped insult after ludicrous insult upon their former pursuer. With the danger well behind them, the whole thing turned into a big laugh. Their faces were red, their sides ached, and their mouths were gaped wide, howling in triumph. Chase never caught a glimpse of the stolen wallet that protruded slightly from Jack's pocket, and Jack smiled inwardly as they laughed together.

They drove straight for the next couple of hours. The highway was empty, and they made good time. In front of them the daylight arched lower across the baby blue sky, and they chased the sun. The lines on the pavement slipped continually past: *swip, swip, swip.* Jack's seat was reclined, and his feet, nestled snugly in his tattered Converse, were resting on the dashboard. The air conditioner never worked right, if at all, so their windows were rolled down as they cruised along. The wind swept throughout the vehicle—battering and sauntering about in a friendly way—cooling them both. Their hair was whipped around, but neither of them seemed to care.

It was a good day to be on the road, it was a good day to be free. Chase began to feel all right, to feel at ease. Perhaps all he needed all along was to cast off responsibilities and everything that tied him down. Maybe it was enough in life to only care about ones self, finding ways to have a good time and shrugging off the difficulties. Out here, away from pressures and pointless anxieties, he felt himself begin to smile. Finally, he was the master of his own destiny. His conscience was quiet, a muffled whisper fading away.

It was nearing six o'clock as they entered Rapid City. The area was gorgeous, and with just over 60,000 people, it was a respectable little community. They stopped for dinner at Quizno's, and as they sat down, Jack called his friend Neal.

"Hey, man. It's Jack. What's up?" He spoke into the mouthpiece smiling. "Oh, yeah? How long till you get off then?" He paused, listening. "Could we just drop by the house early? Oh, yeah. I met this guy on the road, he's our age, and he gave me a lift. A pretty cool kid," Jack said, giving Chase playful wink. "Oh ... okay. So I guess we'll see you at nine then. Yeah, it's cool. We'll just hang out and check out the town or something. All right, man, peace."

He hung up the phone and sat across the table, giving Chase a sarcastically flustered look.

"Bad news?" Chase asked.

"Ah, no," Jack said, brushing the question off with a flip of his hand. "We just have to kill an hour or two before we head over to Neal's house. He's at work right now, and the house is all locked, so we can't just chill over there. So, yeah, whatever ... we'll just walk around and see what this place has to offer," he finished, turning his attention to the food at hand.

They quickly consumed their meals and set off for a look around. The city was small, and had a touristy feel to it. Various small shops lined the street as they walked along. Chase pulled out a cigarette, his first in several hours, and offered one to Jack, who accepted. They sauntered along the sidewalks–not talking much, except to point out various stores that looked interesting. The warmth of the day radiated off the pavement, and the oppressive evening heat sweltered tempestuously around them. Eventually as they walked along, they passed by a strip club.

"Bummer it's a twenty-one and up club," Jack said, looking disappointed. "No worries, though, we'll have plenty of action tonight." Jack turned to walk away, but Chase stood unmoving, looking up at the sign hanging above the tinted windows.

What's the point in this? Chase thought as he walked along. *It's like I'm trapped in a play. We're all just running through a script. It's not enough. I just want to be okay. I know I've been happy before . . . but it never lasts. Why is that? I can't force myself to be all right. I just can't. I keep sinking. Is doing what's right the way to happiness? Is the majority the judge of right and wrong? Porn is looked down on by many . . . but looked at by many and more . . . Does that matter? Is society becoming more and more twisted and infected by something?*

He was walking through a suburb of downtown Chicago late at night. His hands were in his sweatshirt pouch, and his arms were pressed against his sides in an effort to contain heat. It was a Saturday night. His parents assumed he was out somewhere with friends, but he had driven to Chicago to escape to somewhere different. Chase liked the city. In the suburbs people put on their masks. They were fake and superficial. They tended to look away when they met eyes with a stranger. Their lawns were always green and trimmed. *It's as if,* he mused as he walked, *they've always been told that to get the house with the little front yard, the yellow SUV and minivan out front, and that white picket fence: now that's success! They got what they wanted! They did it... right? Of course they did! They would assure themselves, resting ill at ease—hidden among everybody else...*

As Chase waited at an intersection, he looked to his right across the street and saw it. "Nancy's Show Girls" it was called. On another night he might have kept on walking. Instead, he turned toward it. The sign on the door read "Eighteen and over." He opened the door and went inside.

There was a short hallway and a man standing behind a counter who took his entrance fee and handed him a ticket.

"What do I do with this?" Chase asked, having never been to a strip club before.

"Take it to the juice bar, and they'll give you a drink. As long as you have that drink in your hand, and it doesn't run out, then you're fine. If you drink it all, you have to pay for another one," he said, waving Chase through.

Chase took a breath and walked into the main room. The lighting was somewhat dim with a crimson tinge to it. Smoke hung heavily in the air, but he didn't notice it much. The room was fairly large, with the juice bar against the far wall and several pool tables off to the side. Accentuating the opposite wall was a platform with a pole running down the center. A few men sat watching a girl lazily slide up and down—flipping her hair sensuously to the music. Lounging against the bar were several girls, and a small array of diverse customers. The guys ranged anywhere from men in cheap business suits to teens no older than himself. As he started toward the bar, the girls' heads turned in his direction, in order to appraise this newcomer. All in all, so far Chase was surprised to find a lack of activity in the club. It wasn't as exciting as he had imagined it to be.

He handed the girl behind the counter his ticket, got his drink, and decided to look around a bit more. There was another hallway near the bar; he headed down it. There were private rooms lining each of the walls. Some of them were empty with the doors opened, so he looked inside. The rooms were grungy, each with its own tattered, old easy chair. Chase grimaced a bit as he thought of all the guys who had sat in those same chairs. He turned, and as he was walking back, he saw a room with the door only partially shut with someone in the middle of a lap dance. Embarrassed, he quickly dropped his eyes. He shuffled back into the main room next to the juice bar, and one of the girls sprawled over her chair spoke to him.

"Looking for something?" she asked.

"Uh," Chase stammered, his cheeks flaring up, "Well, uh," he continued, "I've never actually been to a strip club before ... so, yeah, I don't know what to do." He laughed nervously, trying to disperse his self-conscious discomfort.

"Oh!" She cried out, sounding pleased. "I see, and what exactly are you looking for? A lap dance? A private show?"

"Well, what do they entail?" he asked, still feeling a bit awkward.

She went on to tell him about the price, and the amount of time he would get in each situation. He was surprised at the amount for the private show—that was until she mentioned that the lines on what was and wasn't allowed were somewhat "blurred." In the end, he opted for the three-minute lap dance.

"Great!" she replied. "Who would you like?"

Chase looked along the bar at his options. They were all dressed in tight fitting clothing and were heavily caked in make up. None of them struck him as very attractive, and he was beginning to regret his impulsiveness. But it was too late to leave now; it was too humiliating. He would go through with the lap dance. He chose the girl who he had been talking to, simply because she seemed nice.

They entered one of the vacant rooms, and she instructed him to sit down. The song began, and she started stripping to the music. Chase was more than uncomfortable at this point, feeling as though there was something wrong with this event. Slowly, as she undressed before him, he grew more and more repulsed. It wasn't her physical appearance that repulsed him; instead it was his own choice to be there. He saw himself as something vile. He was ashamed of his own actions. A sickening awareness of his own moral vagueness filtered through his mind. *What am I doing here? What am I hoping to find?* It made Chase feel beaten and empty. Nausea began to creep up from the pit of his stomach.

Desperately, in an attempt to escape the shrieking of his conscience, he talked to the girl. He started babbling, asking how long she had been working there, why she did it, what her plans were down the road, and so on. She was so close to him, but he had never felt so frantically alone. The girl stared at him with a queer expression, searching his tormented eyes for the point in his forced banter. Deciding that he was nervous, and seeing as it was his first time, she politely indulged his questioning—even smiling as she answered. Then, all of a sudden, the song was over. She stepped away from him, pulling her clothing on without giving him the slightest notice, and said, "Well, hope you enjoyed yourself. Come back anytime."

Then she smiled, a quick and required smile, promptly leaving the room. The deal was over. Her business obligation was fulfilled. Chase stayed sitting for a minute after she left, trying to collect himself. *What is wrong with me?* he thought. *Don't most guys get excited about this stuff?* Chase could not shake the filth he felt on himself. He stared up at the single bulb in the ceiling, which seemed to glare down at him. *Aren't you satisfied?* it seemed to taunt.

He stumbled from the chair into the bathroom, feeling like he would be sick. Somehow, he held the convulsions back, and standing in front of the mirror, he washed his face—thoroughly splashing the tepid tap water onto his tired features. As he glanced into the mirror, he saw himself as a creature driven and derided by hopelessness, and his eyes burned with anguish and shame.

People were already beginning to arrive at Neal's party as they pulled into the wide, sweeping double entrance driveway. A large, pearl-colored house stood before them. An upper balcony stretched above, hugging the walls. The windows were long and crisply sparkled back at them. Chase was taken aback by the stunning grandeur of the place.

"This is his parents' house right?" asked Chase as he stared in dumb amazement up at the house.

"Well, it's one of several, actually." Jack laughed. "His parents are living elsewhere this summer, so he pretty much has the place to himself for the next three months. Tight, huh? Come on, let's head inside and see what's up."

They joined the swarming mass of bodies as they entered. The party had only just started, but already there were well over a hundred people circulating through the house's interior. Jack led through groups of girls decked out in their finest, who huddled together whispering, laughing, and eying different attractive guys. Groups of guys stood around laughing and betting on who would score. Pulsing over everything was the steady beat of the stereo. It was a scene from any or all teen movies. As they walked into the living room, someone yelled out.

"Jack! Get over here!"

It was Neal. Jack's face lit up as he saw his college buddy, and he bounded over the couch at him, practically knocking them both over. Chase stood by as they eagerly exchanged greetings. Neal leaped up on a coffee table and yelled at the room.

"Everybody! Hey, this is my roommate, Jack. He hitchhiked from Orlando to get here!"

At this, everyone in the room let out a round of applause, and Jack stood smiling and waving back at everyone. Chase continued standing nearby.

"Hey, let's head onto the balcony for some drinks," Neal said as he climbed down from his perch.

"Sounds good," Jack replied. And then, as if seeing Chase for the first time, he added, "Hey, Neal. This is the guy who gave me a ride today. His name is Chase."

"Oh, excellent!" Neal exclaimed, shaking hands with Chase. "I dig it man—that's where it is, just out there driving and picking up a complete stranger. Right on ... right on."

They detached themselves from the groups of random people and headed out onto the balcony. Neal walked over to a cooler, pulled out a bottle of Malibu rum, and mixed three cups for them. He held up his cup as a toast.

"To you guys! And to having one hell of a party!"

Jack hollered in assent, and they both threw back their cups. Chase paused for some reason and sat looking at the drink in his hand. He saw a distorted image of himself reflected back from the pooled surface. This crude, gawking reflection stared right back—mocking, taunting. Drinking was a medication for him, lulling him away as it numbed his pain. Sitting there holding the cup, he suddenly felt sick about it all. He hated that he would rather drink alone than with others.

"Hey, what's the matter?" Jack asked. "Kill that shot!"

"Um, I'm actually not too fond of rum," Chase mumbled.

"Oh give me a break! Finish it!" Jack and Neal shouted in unison.

"Uh, I uh..."

"You've gotta be kidding me! Man up, and take it already!"

Chase tried protesting again, and once again he was quickly shot down. He sat still, embarrassed, and feeling hot-red humiliation shooting up his face. He was just about to take a drink when they grew bored of his company, and walked down to join the rest of the party shaking their heads, and Jack apologizing for bringing him.

Shame hit Chase like a wave of nausea. He was fiercely embarrassed. Desperation at his failure to make a good impression and fit in rolled over him. He snatched up the cup, spilling some over the edge, and downed it in a single gulp. Then he ran over and opened up a bottle of 151, taking a long pull from it. Straight hard liquor cascaded down his waiting throat, burning all the way down. He shook his head, grimacing at the alcohol's acrid sting. He didn't care anymore; he just wanted to lose himself in the night. Grabbing a beer, he walked downstairs.

The party was in full swing now. A mass of people were dancing and grinding up against one another in the living room and out near the pool deck. People cheered as guys raced at shotgunning their beers. An intense game of beer pong took up the dining area, and the kitchen was packed with people moving in and out to get more drinks. Chase stumbled around, not yet feeling the alcohol's effects, and bumped into Jack, who was in the middle of downing a load from the beer bong.

"Hey, look who finally decided to join the party!" Jack said, passing the end to Chase. "Drink up!"

Eager to not disappoint Jack again, Chase took the end and chugged another beer. Jack got everyone cheering, and soon Chase had downed another two shots. Then the liquor finally caught up and hit him like a freight train.

"Whoa, it's hot in here!" Chase yelled, pulling his shirt off and falling down all in the same instant.

A wave of blurred faces circled around him laughing. They pulled him up, and started messing with him.

"Ha ha. Get a look at this guy."

"Fool can hardly stand!"

"Hey, bro, how many fingers am I holding up?"

"Ha ha—did you see that? That dude totally just ran into the wall! And look at that stupid grin on his face! Priceless!"

"He's gunna be hurtin' tomorrow."

"Dude, you are so drunk right now."

"I'm no drunnnnkk..." Chase dumbly protested. "Noooo drinky much much."

Everyone laughed and the party rolled on. Soon he couldn't stand up anymore, and everyone trickled back to their own things and forgot about him. He lay there alone, half asleep and stupidly staring up at the ceiling mumbling to himself: "That light, that way...it shines outward...in circles...look—ha ha, loooook...why..."

His stomach began to protest. The drinks, now all mixed together, permeated his insides tying them into knots. Rotten nausea enveloped his body. He writhed on the ground in misery, trying to get up and go to the bathroom. No one paid him any attention as he tried standing. He made it to his feet just as his stomach began to reject its contents. It shot up his throat in an acidic wave, rushing out his mouth and onto the carpet.

"What the hell?" Someone nearby him yelled out.

Chase couldn't keep track of anything anymore. The room spun uncontrollably, causing him to vomit again. Hands were grabbing him now. He felt himself being carried along; a shot of fresh air hit him in the face. He was outside. He felt himself grow sick again. He doubled up, retching, but nothing came out. Voices were swearing next to him. He was dropped heavily on the ground outside. He felt the pain, and for an instant a feeling of hate shot through him. Then as quickly as it had come it left again, leaving him once more in a lethargic stupor. Footsteps faded away. He was alone.

Chase lay on the ground for a long time trying not to move. He willed himself to just fall asleep so that he could get rid of the pain in his gut. It was no good. The world was spinning wildly around him. He was aware of his physical discomfort, and was unable to shake it off. As the minutes rolled past, and the night air lost its warmth, he realized that he was shaking. He hugged his arms against his body and tucked his legs up as best he could. It did little to help. The cold seeped in, covering him in a bitter blanket. No one came out to help him. He lay alone on the hard ground, slowly drifting off to sleep.

MIRIAM

The pungent aroma of beer and vomit floated into Chase's nostrils, wrestling him back from fitful dreams and memories. He lay staring at the blades of grass in front of his blurred vision.

"What the ... ?" he murmured softly, trying to sit up.

The sun was beginning its daily ascent, just cresting the far off tree line. Littered cups and bottles from the night before laid scattered across the lawn. Two other people lay nearby under a blanket. Their clothes were strewn about.

"At least someone had a good night," Chase thought, as he tried gaining his balance.

Where am I?

Chase looked around the yard and then up at Neal's house. He was at a party. He had come here with Jack. Oh, yeah, Jack. Where was Jack? He swore furiously to himself. *He left me out here,* he thought.

Chase paused to check his pockets for his wallet and keys. They were both still there. *Good*, he thought, *at least I'm still all right.* He had a splitting headache, and the sunlight did little to improve his mood. He stumbled toward the front of the house, taking the side gate so as to not run into anyone. Finding his car where he had left it, he climbed inside. There was a car parked on either end of him, leaving him only inches of clearance on each side. He swore under his breath. It took him almost five minutes of inching back and forth before he was able to free his car from the tight, little nook. He slowly backed the car out, and when successfully out of the driveway, he whipped out onto the street and screeched away. He stared straight ahead and didn't look back.

The clock on the radio read 9:47 am. Chase fumbled in the glove compartment and snagged a pair of tinted sunglasses. He gratefully put them on. Finally he was able to open his eyes to the harsh morning sunlight. He drove slowly across town, trying to find his bearings. His head was pulsing, each beat like a war drum inside his sensitive skull. He slumped at the wheel, gently drifting into the other lane.

Honk! The horn of an oncoming car bleated out, knocking him back into reality. A shot of adrenaline ripped through his body. His eyes shot open, his hands clenched the wheel, and his whole body tensed.

Screw this, he thought, *I need to stop and get some coffee.* Moments later he was pulling into a Denny's on the outskirts of town. As Chase was getting out of the car, he realized part of his shirt was moist. Looking down he discovered that he was drenched in a mixture of dirt, dew, and vomit. Smelling it only confirmed the matter. He cringed, turning his nose away in disgust.

Chase hopped back into the Jeep and changed out of his clothing. He took out a can of body spray and showered himself in it. He glanced at the rearview mirror. He hadn't shaved in a few days, and that combined with his last few days' venture did little to improve his situation. Pausing, he reached back into his bag and grabbed a hooded sweatshirt and pulled it on. He put his hood up, and positioned his glasses back on, then once again hopped out of the car.

His mood was shifting from tired and upset into a mellow gloom. *It doesn't matter much anyway,* he figured, *nothing really matters much.* The swinging door smacked him in the shoulder as he walked in. It barely registered. Then he began to laugh. He stood in the lobby, partially bent over, giving into this fit of pointless laughter. His lips curled into a grin as he tried to hold it in. A waitress nearby looked at him with a queer expression on her face. Several others nearby turned their heads in quiet curiosity. The laughter subsided quickly, and Chase was left feeling refreshed with a slight grin on his face.

The universe is making a mockery of me, Chase thought. *What a wonderfully sick sense of humor! I exist in a bubble of secret secrets and silent laughter. I am me—the great bubble explorer!*

He started laughing again at this ridiculous thought in his tired mind when a waitress walked up, cutting his amusement short.

"Just one?" she asked, twisting the cap on her pen. "Right this way sir."

He followed her to the counter, and sat at one of the stools facing the kitchen. *It's warm inside,* he thought, *or maybe it's just the sweatshirt.*

"What can I get started for ya?" the waitress asked politely.

"Some coffee would be amazing," Chase replied. "And I'm not sure on the food yet."

"All right, well, I'll be back with that in just a minute, and I'll take the rest of your order then."

"Thanks a lot."

What do I want? he pondered. His eyes scanned the menu, mentally tasting each of the dishes he examined. His stomach groaned in apprehension, and his mouth watered. He saw the waitress approaching and made his choice.

"Here you are," she said, pouring a cup in front of him and setting the pot down. "Have you decided on anything?"

"Yes, I'll have the sausage omelet with a side of hash browns," Chase replied right away.

The waitress took down his order and then spun around and was off on her way. *I wonder if she enjoys her work?* The thought ran across his mind. *What makes someone like or dislike their job? Money can't be the only factor, and the importance of a job can't be the only thing.* This random debate continued to bounce around his head as he absently picked up his cup and slurped on the warm beverage. He let out a satisfied sigh, gazing into his cup with relaxed indifference.

The food arrived several minutes later, piping hot and steaming with pleasurable aromas. Chase ate quickly, his taste buds urging him on. When he was finished he paid his bill, left a tip, and headed out the door.

Squinting as he walked outside, Chase fumbled around in his pockets until he found his keys. His head still throbbed, so he took two Advil from his glove compartment and chewed and swallowed them without water.

"Time to get out of this place," he mumbled to himself.

He pulled a road map from under the seat and skimmed it over. The westbound interstate was close by, and he pulled out, veering toward it. Chase was behind the wheel and on the road again.

The highway was fairly deserted save for a few trucks rolling along. Chase cruised at around eighty miles per hour, thinking about what the last two days had brought. It was comforting, in a weird sort of way, to be out on his own. His newly gained freedom pleased him, but still the restlessness was there. It invaded every corner of his being, tugging him in all directions in search of... in search of what? He still didn't know. *Am I going to find it?* he thought. *Or just waste some time and gas? Well... as long as I've got money and a road I'll keep going. Money...*

Chase suddenly realized he didn't know how much money he had left. He reached into his back pocket and pulled his wallet out. Driving with his knees, he counted up the bills.

"Twenty, forty, sixty," he counted aloud to himself. "One hundred forty, one hundred sixty, one hundred and sixty five... one hundred and sixty seven..."

He stared down at the money in his hands and then counted it again to make sure he was right. There was no mistaking it; he had about half the amount of money he had started with two days earlier.

"What the ... ? How in the world did I go through that much money so fast?" He asked himself, feeling genuinely amazed.

He tallied up the number of meals he had bought, and the number of times he had stopped to get gas. It all added up. *Dang,* he thought, *money is practically flying out the window! I'm going to have to cut back a bit on basic expenses. Insane. Simply insane,* he thought, shaking his head.

The Wyoming countryside lulled past him outside his windows. He did not remember crossing the border, but his head had been all over the place that morning. He pulled out a cigarette and rolled down the window an inch. The wind ripped cruelly throughout the interior of the car until Chase rolled it back up, deciding to use an empty bottle as an ashtray. It was almost noon, but he didn't feel like stopping anywhere to eat, so he kept driving on.

The highway split in two different directions, and Chase followed the one leading west toward Boise. It was a small highway, with only two lanes heading in each direction. His cigarette burned down, so he lit another. He exhaled a cloud of smoke and stared thoughtfully at it. He watched the way it streamed out, blurring the scene in front of him before dissipating into thin air. He thought about Jack and about being drunk the night before. *Why do I feel the need to smoke and drink?* he wondered. *Even when I sometimes want to stop, I can't make myself.* He paused. *It's true, though ... I make the choice. There is no denying that I see both sides, but in the end always give in to these wants. My spirit is always overcome ... and it's by choice! Why can't I choose what is better for me?* Chase raged.

There is something flawed inside of me, he slowly reasoned. *I don't feel right. It's as if I'm sick somehow ... Is there really anything decent inside me? I can sit back and judge others easily enough, but what am I? There is something wrong with me.*

Chase was completely zoned out. He felt himself on the verge of something, and all his concentration was focused on his inner dilemma. He failed to notice when the lane he was in bent off to the right, while the highway went on. He also failed to see the jagged, baseball-sized rock, sunning itself in his lane. Chase hit the rock going just under sixty miles per hour.

What happened next lasted only a few seconds, but to Chase time stopped moving. The rock punctured a hole in his left front tire, completely blowing it out. The car lurched left, knocking Chase out of his train of thought and into the nightmare shock of the moment. He squeezed the steering wheel, struggling to get a grip on his situation. Nothing made sense. *What's happening? Where am I?* These thoughts flashed through his mind in the same instant as his body reacted instinctively to the situation. His hands wrenched the wheel to the right, trying to bring the car back in line. He ended up overcompensating. The car careened to the right. Half his car was now over the white line and running through the gravel off the roads edge. He slammed down the brakes without thinking, causing the Jeep to fishtail back and forth across the road. Chase opened his mouth, but no sound came out. Random thoughts and images shot through his mind: *Playing in a sandbox. Family and friends at a picnic on the lake. The sun setting in the summer. Rum, weed, ecstasy, cigarettes, coke. Mushroom cloud. A fish jumping. High school graduation. Laughing. Waterfalls. Raindrops. Fear.*

His car was in the middle of a complete spin. There was nothing he could do. He yanked at the steering wheel trying anything to regain control, but just then he felt something break. The steering wheel was useless. He was heading off the road with no control. There was a fence and a telephone pole next to it. The driver's side of the car was spinning in a collision course with the pole. In the complete desperation and terror of the moment, he screamed out the first thing that came to his head:

"*God, save me!*"

Chase squeezed his eyes shut. Every muscle in his body was tense and waiting for the impact. His car skidded bumpily to a stop. Then it was silent. Chase forced his eyes open. His whole body was shaking. Jittering, he pried his hands from the wheel and looked out the window. There he sat, inches away from the telephone pole, which only seconds before threatened to crush the life from him. Chase exhaled. He had not realized he was holding his breath. His body fell limp in the seat as he leaned back, staring up at the ceiling. He closed his eyes, breathing deeply the sweet, sweet air. As he lay there, he heard a tapping on his window.

Chase looked up to find that he was staring into the face of a stranger. The stranger appeared to be rather good-sized, with trim, muscular arms. His head was bald, and he had a five o'clock shadow lightly peppered on his face. He stared inside with concern showing in his eyes. Chase reached out and wound down the window.

"Are you all right, son?" the stranger asked earnestly.

"I think so," Chase replied trying to focus. "Just a bit shook up."

"You're lucky. I saw the whole thing as I was driving this way. You damn near smashed in the whole side of your car on that pole—I can't believe you stopped in time. That was some luck."

"Yeah, some luck..." Chase mumbled.

"You'll have to get a tow truck, can't be sure everything's all right until you get it all checked out," the man said. "Do you live around here?"

"No, I live in I live in Illinois. I'm on my way to visit relatives in Oregon," he lied.

"Well listen, since you're not from around here, I'd be happy to help you out. You can have it towed to my place, and I can help you fix whatever's wrong with it. I'm Lance, by the way," he said extending his hand.

"Chase," he said, shaking Lance's outstretched hand.

It took about thirty-five minutes before the tow truck arrived, and when it did, it took another twenty minutes or so to get everything straightened out. Lance was very helpful in getting everything settled, and before long Chase was sitting in the passenger seat of Lance's pickup heading out. The tow truck driver followed close behind.

"Yeah, your alignment seems to be all jacked up," Lance was saying. "We'll take a look at it all when we get back. I'm fairly handy with cars, so hopefully we'll be able to deal with any problems we discover."

"Thanks a lot. I mean, really, it helps a lot. I'd hate to have to worry my parents with any of this, so hopefully nothing major comes up."

"Oh it's all right, don't worry yourself over it. You're more than welcome to stay with us till you get everything straightened out, and hopefully within a day or two you'll be on your way."

"Sounds great," Chase said feeling very relieved to have landed in such fortunate circumstances.

Lance lived on the outskirts of a place called Rock Springs, which wasn't far from the interstate. As they pulled down the gravel driveway, Chase gathered in his new surroundings. There was a small blue house sitting next to a larger metal building that looked to be some sort of shop. Just below the house, down a slight hill, there stood a barn with a fenced off area attached to it. There were trees growing along the property, and several goats were ambling about in the thicket. They pulled up to a wide parking area next to the house and got out. The tow truck driver asked where to put the car, then backed it in and dropped it down.

"That'll be sixty-five dollars," the driver said as he climbed out of the cab.

Chase grimaced when he heard the price, but took out the money and paid him. The tow truck driver tipped his head, climbed back into the truck, and was off.

"We'll look it over this evening after dinner," Lance said. "Let's head inside and freshen up a bit before it's time to eat."

Chase followed him inside. He suddenly realized that he had not showered in the last three days and was immediately embarrassed. He rushed back to the Jeep and grabbed his bag with clothes in it; then he caught up with Lance and stepped inside.

Chase stared around as he entered the house. Immediately noticeable were the two mounted deer heads hanging on the wall, as well as a stuffed duck strung up. Chase made a mental note of this, thinking it wise to pay attention to his host's interests, if only for something to talk about. In the kitchen, Lance's wife was busy preparing dinner.

"Hon, this is Chase," Lance said introducing them. "He got into an accident back near the highway and is going to stay with us until we can get his car up and running smoothly again."

"Nice to meet you, Chase. I'm Susan." She put out her hand and shook Chase's.

"Nice to meet you too, and thank you both so much."

"Oh, it's no problem, dear. Just make yourself at home," Susan said.

"I'm sorry to press, but is it possible for me to take a shower?" Chase asked. "It's been a long day, and I could use one if you don't mind."

"Sure thing, just head down the hall there and hang a left," Susan replied. "Towels are in the drawer."

"Thanks a lot," Chase said as he turned and walked down the hallway following her directions.

The bathroom was nothing fancy, but it had a comfortable feel to it. The whole house was very inviting. It was a house where people weren't afraid to live. There were various bathroom implements scattered about on the counter. The shower curtain was blue with a picture of a whale across it. Chase smiled as he gazed about the room.

"This bathroom has seen a few miles," Chase muttered as he shut the door.

He stripped off his dirty clothing and hopped in the shower. Chase closed his eyes and let the water rush over him—warm droplets bursting and running down his face. He stood still, soaking in the warmth of the shower. It was as much an emotional cleansing as a physical one. The filth and bad taste of the last day and night seemed to run down the drain. He was left feeling refreshed and rejuvenated.

Hopping out of the shower, he toweled off briskly and checked his reflection in the mirror. He had noticeable bags under his eyes from lack of decent sleep, but the eyes themselves were bright and alert. He felt better than he had in several days. A quick smile flashed across his face, and then he spun around and threw some clothes on. He swung the door open and stepped out, bumping into someone. They spun to face each other.

"Well, hello," this new girl said, mildly surprised. "I'm Miriam."

Words failed Chase. He stood there dumbly staring back at her. The girl standing in front of him was stunning. This unexpected meeting took him completely by surprise. She had long, thick brown hair that spilled back over her shoulders. Her hazel eyes danced with life as she stared back at him. She had a sweet, almost bashful smile. Her skin was lightly tanned, and

Chase could detect no signs of makeup on her face, yet she glowed with sweet innocence and complete confidence. She had on only a tank top and jeans, but they showed off the relaxed, self-satisfied attitude she seemed to posses.

"Usually this is the part where you tell me your name," she said smiling.

Chase snapped back.

"Whoa, sorry about that," he said. "Caught me off guard there." He laughed. "I'm Chase."

"Nice to meet you," she said shaking his hand. "I mean, you did almost lay me out, but I'll forgive you this time."

"Hey now," Chase playfully argued back. "I was just minding my own business when you go flying through here like the place was on fire."

They both laughed while staring at each other. After the noise died, they were still standing there. A slight feeling of embarrassment came over each of them, as they both tried speaking at the same time.

"Well, uh, I'm heading that way." Miriam said pointing down the hall. "I guess I'll see you at dinner?"

"Uh, yeah, yep—I'll be there," Chase stammered. "Don't go running into anymore poor bystanders."

"Ha! You better watch yourself kid," she said over her shoulder as she walked off.

Chase stood staring after her for a second as she floated off. *Wow,* he thought. *She's so alive and gor-*

geous. And I'm such a dork... "*Don't run into anymore poor bystanders...* " *Real smooth, Chase, real smooth.* He turned and walked off, criticizing himself for his naïve line and off guard clumsiness.

At the dinner table, Chase cast side-glances at Miriam whenever no one was looking. The meal was excellent: mashed potatoes with fresh green beans, barbequed pork chops, and fluffy rolls on the side. Chase had missed lunch during the course of the day, and was now ravenously hungry. Over the course of dinner, Chase got better acquainted with Miriam and her parents.

"So you're from near Chicago then, Chase?" Susan asked.

"Yeah, I'm not too far away from there. It's a bit smaller of a place," Chase answered.

"I can't believe you're driving all the way to Oregon by yourself," Susan continued. "Why didn't you just fly there?"

"I wanted to see some of the country between here and there. I'm in no rush, so I figured it could be fun," Chase said.

"Oh, but wasn't that ride some fun?" Miriam broke in.

"Ha, yeah sure," Chase laughed back. "I didn't realize Wyoming was such a dangerous place."

"Accidents can happen to anyone," Lance said. "You're just lucky there was no major damage to you or your car."

Yeah, lucky, Chase thought.

There's that word again, Chase pondered. It had been gnawing at the back of his mind ever since the crash. *Was I lucky? I saw the pole heading straight for me ... how did I not crash into it?*

"Would you like any ice cream for desert, Chase?" Susan asked.

"Uh, yes please," he replied. He stood up and helped her clear the dishes, piling them all into the sink.

"Oh, I approve of this one," Susan said

"Just doing what I can," he said slightly blushing.

After dessert, Lance went out with Chase to examine the Jeep. Chase was not the most mechanically inclined person. In fact, if asked how to do anything beyond pumping gas, he would quickly veer to another topic. So while Lance examined the damage, Chase stood by, pretending he knew what was going on. The evening air was setting in, and a light breeze had sprung up. Chase breathed in, relishing the clean, rustic air that filled his nostrils. Lance picked his head up saying, "Yeah, it's what I was guessing—the rack and pinion arm is broken right in half."

"Right ... " Chase said having no idea what Lance was referring to.

"It's the part of your car that makes the wheel turn." Lance said, patiently explaining. "I can fix it, but we need to get the part first. It's too late tonight, but in the morning we'll see what we can do. Right now, though, we can change that blown-out tire. You have a spare, right?"

"Yeah, it's in the back—I'm pretty sure. I've never had to use it before," Chase confessed. "My dad always brings our cars in when something's wrong, so I'm not exactly up to speed on the whole mechanical thing."

"Well that simply won't do," Lance said. "What if you had a flat out on some deserted road? You need to be able to change a tire on your own. All my boys, when they were living at home, had to learn. So that's what you're going to do," he said, smiling. "You get to change it, and I get to critique."

"By myself?" Chase asked, feeling unsettled by the prospect. "What if I break something?"

"I'm right here—you'll do fine. This is something that everyone needs to be able to do. Grab your tire and jack."

Feeling wary about the whole ordeal, Chase walked to the Jeep and opened the back. He dragged the new wheel out, and located the tire jack. He brought both items to the front of the car, and then looked to Lance waiting for instruction.

"What is the first thing we want to do?" Lance asked him.

"Uh … jack up the car?" he guessed.

"We have a winner!" Lance teased. "And you said you didn't know the first thing about cars. Kid, you're a natural." He laughed to himself, and his laughing helped put Chase at ease.

This isn't some huge test, Chase thought. *No one is judging me—it's all good.* He was squatting down trying to figure out where to place the jack, when he heard footsteps coming up behind him. He turned his head, and looked over his shoulder. There was Miriam, walking up and standing next to her dad. She flashed him a quick smile and said, "First time changing a tire, huh?"

"Is it that obvious?" Chase asked.

"Dad made me do it by myself the first time too," she said. "Of course, that was when I was fourteen."

Chase laughed shaking his head.

"Yeah, just rub it in," he said grinning. "Not all of us are so talented."

He bumbled around trying to get the jack set up right before he finally had it in the optimal position. With a silent wish, he began moving the lever up and down. The Jeep groaned as it was shifted from its place. It slowly rose up, and Lance gave him two supports to put under the car once he had it well off the ground. Next, Chase set in with the lug wrench to take off the bolts.

"You do realize," Miriam started saying, "that you're twisting the wrong way right?"

Dang, she's right, Chase thought. He paused, quickly trying to think of witty comeback.

"Oops."

Wow. Yeah, that pretty much sums up my intelligence level at the moment, Chase thought. *"Oops?" Way to go. You're a modern day Shakespeare there, Chase, so very verbally elegant,* he thought, poking fun at himself.

Chase continued to labor away at his current task like a half-trained monkey, and eventually the Jeep sat before him on its new wheel. He stood up feeling satisfied with his accomplishment, glancing over to the others for their approval. Lance looked gravely back at him, making him freeze up. Miriam was also looking curiously at her father. Chase shifted from one foot to the other, waiting for the verdict.

"Uh, well…you do realize that wheel is on backwards…right?" Lance said, trying to point this embarrassing affair out as gently as possible.

The feeling of satisfaction immediately left Chase's face. His shoulders slumped.

"You've got to be…" he started saying, until he saw a grin creep onto Lance's face.

"Ha ha, I'm sorry, son—I couldn't help it," He said. "But the look on your face was just priceless."

"So not cool," Chase said relaxing again. "Is that it then?"

"Yeah, let's head in. Make sure to put your jack away."

Lance turned and headed for the house. Chase went to the back of the car and replaced the tool where he had found it. He turned to head back into the house, and as he spun around there stood Miriam waiting for him. His heart sped up a bit as he walked toward her. A dazzling smile danced across her face as he approached. Chase felt like his insides were melting away. He felt his knees go weak and struggled to compose himself. He smiled back as he caught up with her.

"Hey don't feel too bad," she whispered. "He did the same thing to me the first time I had to change one too. He gets a kick out of hassling people. I think he's really taken a liking to you, though."

"Ha ha. Is that what you'd call it?" he replied, shaking his head. "No, he is a really great guy. I'm grateful to him for everything. You guys are all really hospitable."

"Yeah, if you don't mind a bit of mocking here and there," she said, winking over her shoulder.

That evening the parents sat up and watched the news and various shows to unwind. Chase and Miriam spent that time hanging out in the next room, listening to various songs from her extensive music collection and talking about anything and everything that popped into their minds. They were hitting it off right away, each of them hassling the other over different likes and dislikes in music and movies. Neither of them could express it, but there was some sort of growing connection kindling between them. They felt it but didn't make any mention of the sense of rightness they each felt. It was the faintest whisper in a quiet room, uncatchable. It was as if their hearts were leaping inside of them, realizing something they had never felt before, but at the same time knowing exactly what it was. It was the hint of the miraculous being stumbled upon, the surprise meeting of two matching souls, the expression of belonging between two people.

Chase immediately felt something with Miriam that he had never felt with anyone before. The more they shared with each other, the stronger the feeling became. Was this what he had been missing in his life? He did not know, but he felt that he had stumbled onto something that he had been desperately searching for. He felt his loneliness seeping away, and Chase was enjoying every second he spent in Miriam's company. He wanted to pour out his soul to her, but held back, still fearful and uncertain. But he felt safe and at ease with her. He wanted to tell her everything there was to know about him, but cautioned himself to slow down. The hours flew by as they talked and laughed late into the night, until Lance walked into the dining room where they sat.

"It's getting late, kids. Let's wrap it up and head to bed. Chase, I'll show you where you're sleeping."

They both glanced at the glowing clock on a nearby desk. The tiny blue numbers shone back that it was past eleven-thirty. They had been talking for over three hours. To Chase's mind, it had only been a few minutes. Time had simply melted away, leaving only the two of them and the flame that blazed to life between them.

"Whoa, totally didn't realize what time it was," Chase exhaled. "I guess I'll see you tomorrow then," he said, standing up and smiling at Miriam.

"Most definitely," she affirmed. "You're a pretty cool guy—beside the fact that you don't like Johnny Cash."

"And you're not too bad yourself, even though you wanted to be a monkey as a kid," he said.

"Hey! Not cool!" She laughed along with him. "Every kid wants to be an animal when their little!"

Chase smiled over his shoulder as he walked out. Although he had been awake for hours, and had not slept well, he felt alive and excited inside. When he laid down in bed in the spare room Lance had assigned to him, he found that he simply could not fall asleep. Whenever he closed his eyes, he saw her face. He thought about the things they had said and how he had made her laugh. He thought about her natural beauty and the ease in which she handled herself. *It's strange,* he considered, *that I don't see her like any other girl I've ever known before. I feel connected to her on some other level. I see her ... and we just know each other ... and I love her. I love who she is.* These thoughts and many others coursed through his excited mind. His young brain sought eagerly to revel in the joy his heart had chanced upon. The newness, the rightness, and the awesome strength—it all whirled around in his racing heart. The excitement overwhelmed every other thought.

That night he dreamed of his crash. That brief moment of his complete lack of control revisited his slumbering memory. It was all there: the exploding tire, the locking up of the brakes, the wrenching of the wheel, and the sickening spin when all hope was abandoned.

"God, save me!"

Chase sat up in bed with a start. A cold sweat was pouring down his body. He realized he had been dreaming. The images of the crash rushed quickly back over him. Had that been his scream? He had forgotten about it until now; the shock of the accident and the nearly fatal collision had masked this detail of the crash from his memory. Chase sat thinking over the crash again. Something was very wrong with what had happened. This disturbing feeling of something else sent a shiver over his whole body. Every hair on his body stood rigid as if hit by lightning. *There was no way I should have stopped right beside that telephone pole,* he thought. *Could it be that...* but he couldn't put into coherent thoughts what it was that he was feeling. He lay back down uncomfortably. He stared up at the ceiling for a long time without thinking or moving—just looking. Eventually he slipped back off to sleep.

The faint increase in morning sunlight sneaking into the room through the blinds awakened Chase from his slumber. His eyelids fluttered open to reveal his alien surroundings. He felt exhausted, like he had gotten almost no rest at all. He lay staring out across the room for several seconds before it came to him where he was. Then he sat bolt upright in bed. *Miriam!* he thought. Chase practically flew out of bed; he spun around in the room looking for clean clothes. The best he could do were some worn blue jeans and a red Foo Fighters shirt he had worn once on the trip already. He decided on a shower and on doing a small load of laundry when he got out.

Chase bumbled out of the room, his body not quite keeping up with the alertness of his head. *I'm definitely going to need some coffee this morning,* he realized. As he stumbled doggedly through the living room, Susan greeted him with a warm smile.

"Well hello there, sleepyhead! How are you feeling this morning?"

"Not quite awake yet," he smiled back. "Is it all right if I take a quick shower?" he asked.

"Oh, sure thing," she replied. "I appreciate your courtesy, but you really don't have to ask—just head in if no one else is there. I'll make you something to eat while you're in there. What would you like?"

"Oh, you really don't have to cook anything if you don't want. I'm fine with just cereal and some coffee."

"Honey, it's all right. How about I make up some pancakes?"

"Sounds great," he said.

Chase took a brief shower, eager to meet up with Miriam. After he dried and put on clothes, he rummaged around in his bag for some body spray. Finding a can, he applied the spray over his shirt. *Much better,* he thought. He took a little time to brush his teeth and fix his hair. A five-day scruff was showing on his face, but he decided against shaving it, feeling that it added to his overall look. He took one final glance at the mirror in order to appraise his overall appearance. His light hair was somewhat ruffled and jutting out in places, but Chase liked the chaotic effect it produced. His shirt comfortably framed his torso, accentuating a thin but toned body beneath. The blue jeans he wore were ripped and faded in several places, but they looked as if they had been intentionally bought that way. He shoved his black Converse back into his bag, and exited the bathroom in socked feet.

The tantalizing aroma of buttery pancakes engulfed his senses as he entered the dining room. Chase felt his mouth begin watering.

"That smells amazing!" Chase praised.

"Oh, thank you, and you're right on time. Have a seat. These first three are finished."

Chase took a seat at the table as Susan brought his food over. He happened to glance over at the oven clock, only to discover that it was 11:35 a.m. He did a double take. Just at that moment Miriam came strolling in from outside.

"Well, look who's finally up," she said as she came and sat down at the table.

"Is that clock right?" Chase asked, pointing toward the glowing green numbers.

"Yes, sir," Miriam affirmed. "And while you were snoozing away, I was outside feeding the animals and cleaning up their stalls."

"Hey, quit hassling our guest," Susan broke in. "Poor kid had a long day yesterday, and you have to do those chores anyway;" she scolded.

"I'm just giving him a hard time," Miriam said, winking at Chase.

"Well, just simmer down and have some pancakes," Susan said, as she scooped several onto a plate for her.

They continued making small-talk over brunch. Chase didn't know what the agenda was for the day, so he asked about Lance's whereabouts and what was going on there.

"This morning he mentioned something about checking for the part on his way home tonight so that you guys could put it in when he's home," Susan explained.

"Sounds good," Chase said nodding. "So what is everyone else doing today? Is there anything I can help out with?"

"I'm heading into Rock Springs this afternoon," Miriam answered. "I'm just going to do a little shopping and drop off a job application. Do you want to come along? I can show you around for the fun of it—plus, it beats sitting around here all day."

"That would be pretty cool," Chase agreed.

"Sweet, we'll leave after I get changed."

While Miriam went to get dressed, Chase helped clear the dishes. He did it absentmindedly, for he was busy thinking about spending more time with Miriam. His mind pictured ideal scenarios for the afternoon. He stopped abruptly at his task, a dirty plate still in hand. For the first time in a long time, he realized that he was happy—that he was hopeful. *I have a chance here,* he thought, *a chance to feel right again. There is such a thing as happiness out there. I just have to be careful not to let it slip away.*

The weight of the situation made him tense up. *I can't afford to lose this,* he thought. *Not now, not now that*

I finally have a taste of something better. Then he began to worry. His mind spun wildly over all the things that could go wrong. He began overanalyzing everything from the night before. Had he misinterpreted the feelings? Had she really been giving off the vibe that he thought she had? Was she like this with everyone, or was there something underlying in the midst of it all? Chase felt his stomach begin to knot up. He was seized by the anxiety that he had misread all the signs. This extreme sense of paranoia plagued his thoughts mercilessly. He hurriedly went to the bathroom and locked the door.

"Get a hold of yourself," he fiercely whispered in the empty room. "Just calm down."

He sat on the lowered porcelain seat staring down at the floor, trying to get the world to make sense. *I'm not always depressed,* he thought. *There are good days— days when I can taste the sunlight on my tongue, or stare in awe at the beauty of life. I am not going to let myself be controlled by my own emotions. I can will these feelings away. I can do it by myself. I'm in control.*

Chase slapped his cheeks several times, shaking his head free of the creeping anxieties of failure. He stood briskly and stared at his reflection in the mirror as if challenging the reflection to fall apart. He turned on the tap water and scooped the cool stream into his hands—splashing the droplets onto his face. *Here goes nothing,* he thought.

The drive into town was very enjoyable. Miriam pointed out various landmarks to Chase, and he asked questions or poked fun at the country scenery. They were nearing town when Chase suddenly blurted out:

"Whoa! Stop!"

"What?" Miriam cried out. "What's wrong?"

"Do you see that tree right there?" he said, pointing off in the direction of the adjacent field. "That's the biggest tree I've ever seen!"

The tree stood by itself out in the field, its skin cracked and rugged from years of solitary guardianship of its section of land. It stretched its summer-tanned limbs to the sky. Branches, as big around as a small car, protruded from its trunk. Chase stared in wonder at the ancient giant.

"We have to climb that," Chase said, as he stared at the trees massive stature.

"What?" Miriam asked somewhat confused.

"We have time," Chase said, averting his eyes back toward Miriam. "Quick, let's pull over and go climb it! I guarantee it'll be fun," he said smiling at her.

Miriam laughed at Chase's excitement. She stole a quick glance at him as they pulled off the road. Chase caught her gaze, and she quickly looked away. It didn't matter, though, because Chase saw the brief shimmer that had rippled through her eyes. It had been there— he was sure of it.

They pulled over and exited the car. Chase led the way as they climbed carefully over the barbwire fence. Chase turned and helped Miriam over the fence (although she was in little need of help), and soon they were running through the field. They paused in the shadow of the tree, and then, turning and smiling at one another, they approached its trunk. The lowest branch was at least two feet over their heads, but Chase was not to be deterred. He turned to Miriam and offered her his hands as a foot stool. She propelled off his locked finger hold, and with a little bit of a push and a pull, she was comfortably seated on the lowest of the rugged branches.

"How will you get up?" she called down, laughing.

"No worries, back when I played in the NBA, I dunked on hoops twice that tall!" he joked, as he stepped back and then charged the tree.

His first attempt at thrusting himself off the trunk and catching the branch ended in comical failure when his fingers slipped off of the branch, and he landed flat on his backside. Miriam could not help but burst out laughing at the hilarious attempt.

"Are you all right?" she cried down through fits of uncontrollable laughter.

Chase lay on his back, caught his breath, and then laughed along with her. The embarrassment he felt was overcome by the overall hilarious effect of the situation. They each lay where they were laughing together. Chase finally sat up, brushing himself off.

"Alrighty then," he said, "attempt *numero dos!*"

This time he was successful at gaining a grip on the limb, and proceeded to haul himself onto the branch.

"Ha! Showed you, ya dumb branch," he said.

Miriam smiled and laughed along with him. They were both enjoying the newness of this adventure. The climbing became effortless after that first branch; the knotted limbs grew closer together making it much easier to ascend. Eventually they settled on a branch about halfway up the tree, a branch where the field below could be viewed through a clear spot in the foliage. They sat there talking and staring down at the scenery below.

"You have to stop by here again on your way back from Portland," Miriam said. "Have some good food, get made fun of by my dad, and come climb trees with me!"

"See you? Well I don't know…" he responded.

"Oh! That's how it is, huh?" she replied, giving him a slight push. "Well maybe you can just walk back to my house, ever think of that buddy?"

"No, no, no!" he cried. "Just kidding, you know I couldn't pass up the chance to hang out with you—it's definitely been the highlight of my trip."

"Oh, your flattery won't work on me. I know how it is," she flirted back. "Just use me for my house and food—that's all I'm good for."

"No way," he said, leaning over and tickling her lightly on the side. "You're amazing. Hanging out with you is great."

She smiled back at him, lightheartedly blocking his tickle attempts. They sat there quietly then, leaning against one another and looking out over the field—each of them wondering the same thing, each of them lost in thoughts of the other. Their hands bumped against each other, and their fingers, as if acting on their own, intertwined delicately together. Chase felt his heart leap inside his chest. There actually was something there—he could barely contain his happiness. Neither one of them wanted to leave, they both wanted to just stay together there all day, but just then Miriam's phone rang, shattering the moment. They parted hands quickly as she dug through her pockets for the phone.

"Sorry," she said.

"Oh, no it's fine," Chase replied. He leaned back against the trunk of the tree and absently listened to the phone conversation.

"Hey, Mom...no actually we stopped to climb a tree." She laughed. "Yeah I know, ha ha...pick up some flour and fruit? What kind?...Oh, okay. Is that all?...All right, sounds good...yep...yeah all right, see ya." Miriam closed the phone and leaned back against the tree.

"Should we get going?" Chase asked, stretching out his arms and back.

"I guess," she replied.

They made their way down the tree, and walked back to the car side by side, bumping into one another as they went along. It was nearing two o'clock. The sun beat down hotly in the in the early afternoon as they hopped in the car and drove the last two miles into town.

The town was not incredibly large, and as they drove through it heading toward the one mall-like shopping center, Chase took in the sights and the homey feel of the place. A lot of the buildings were old and made of brick, but they were balanced by the new, droll buildings that sat without any feel of character along the spaces that flanked the plain sidewalks. Small groups of people walked down the main street, some strolling just to stroll and others bustling from store to store. There was nothing astounding about the place to Chase. As it was, he was paying more attention to Miriam than to his surroundings. He was lost in the soft curves of her face. Whenever she glanced over and flashed him a full, bright smile, he felt his insides almost floating. Her hair tossed in the breeze, tumbling down her neck and shoulders whenever she laughed. Chase could hardly sit still; he wanted to run, dance, sing! *All is well with the world!* he thought. He could not believe how lucky he was to be sitting there with her.

They pulled in at a plaza, and the shopping began. They went from clothes store to clothes store trying on anything and everything. Chase, who usually detested shopping, found himself having such a good time that he paid no attention whatsoever to the amount of time they spent running around. They each picked out crazy outfits that the other had to try on, and more often than not, random people in the store pitched in their own opinions on how they looked.

"Oh, those pink pants are so *you!*" A lady shopping in the store remarked to Chase as he modeled the outfit Miriam picked out.

"Yep, have to agree," Miriam weighed in. "You have to get them now," she said.

"I don't know," Chase said gravely. "Does my butt look all right?" he asked, posing like a seasoned runway model.

They all laughed together as he put on a show, strolling with audacious poise down the aisle, twirling and winking seductively at anyone near him. It was all great fun, and before long, they had attracted quite the crowd. Everyone whooped and clapped as they each took turns modeling their array of mismatch clothing. At the end, they both walked out together, and took a bow holding hands.

As the crowd dispersed, Miriam caught a glimpse of someone she knew looking at her and talking into his cell phone before he dissolved into the crowd and out of view. Chase saw the worried look written on her face and asked what was wrong.

"Nothing," she replied, trying to brush off his question.

Chase could tell something was wrong, though, and persisted delicately.

"I just saw someone, my ex-boyfriend's best friend. I broke up with my ex just before school ended, and it was a nasty break up."

"Not fun," Chase answered. "Why'd you two break up?"

"He cheated on me, actually," she said, "with one of my friends."

Chase grimaced.

"Wow," he said. "I'm really sorry, but you definitely deserve way better."

"Thanks," she replied. "You don't need to apologize—it's not your fault or anything. He really was horrible, so finally I broke up with him. Problem is, though, that he has been trying to get back together with me for the last month now, and I'm fed up with it. He's a real jerk."

"Yeah, no kidding," Chase agreed. "How long did you two date?"

"Like around eight months. He was cheating on me for three of them."

Chase shook his head in amazement. He could not understand how anyone could ever cheat on Miriam. At the same time though, he was secretly happy for the chance it gave him. *His loss,* he thought. *If I ever get the chance, there is no way I'll ever do anything to hurt her. I'd give anything to make her happy.*

"Come on. I'll buy you a milkshake," Chase said with a smile, throwing his arm around her shoulder.

"Deal," she agreed laughing.

They walked arm-in-arm across the street to an ice cream shop. They were both joking around as they entered the shop, but Miriam halted as they entered. Sitting across the room was Max, her ex-boyfriend, and two of his friends

"Is that him?" Chase whispered, eyeing the biggest one in the group.

"Yeah," she replied. "Whatever, lets just go."

"Sure," he answered, "right after we get our milkshakes."

He smiled audaciously and walked over to the counter, his arm draped loosely over her shoulders. Out of the corner of his eye he sized up her ex. He was very athletic looking, with broad, muscular shoulders and short spiked hair. He looked just a little over six feet tall, and he wore a tank top—allowing Chase to get a good look at his muscles, which were tensed and not so very tiny. Max sat there glaring daggers at Chase, his jaw clenched in apprehension. Chase ordered their milkshakes, and as they were walking out, he turned and looked Max straight in the eye, curled the outside edge of his lip up, and winked at him.

Max leapt up right away, and with his friends hot on his heels, followed Chase and Miriam out into the parking lot. Chase smiled inwardly as he saw him getting up. His baiting had worked. The parking lot next to the ice cream store was empty, and cars driving by had a poor view of anything. The arena was set.

"Hey! Miriam!" Max yelled out from behind them as they were walking through the lot.

"Crap," Miriam whispered under her breath. "Let me take care of this, all right? He has a bad temper, and he might take it out on you—please just let me talk to him."

"Max, we're busy," she said. "We have errands we need to run. I can't talk right now."

"This won't take long," he argued. "I just want to talk to you alone for a minute."

"I told you," she repeated, "we're busy. If you want to talk, you can call me later."

She turned her back on him to walk away, but Max walked over yelling after her. "I said I want to talk to you," he spat, "so wait a minute."

Chase had been quiet up until this point, but hearing him yell at her that way made his blood boil like molten in his veins. He didn't care that this guy had a good thirty pounds on him; if he made one move at Miriam, Chase was going to put him in the hospital. This mixture of anger and adrenaline ran through his body, Chase drank it up until he was inebriated with it. He stepped in front of Max, cutting off his advance toward Miriam.

"You'd better back up, man. She said she doesn't want to talk to you."

Max's face flushed crimson red, a mixture of embarrassment and anger. He paused briefly, pretended to turn around, then cocked back his fist and swung around with all his might seeking to knock Chase's head clear off his body. Time seemed to almost stop for Chase. He saw the knotted fist swinging toward his face and deftly ducked as the blow rushed just inches over his head. Chase now had his legs bent on the ground, and using the force from his bent limbs, he sprung off the ground with his fist clenched in front of him. Max, who had been thrown off balance from his miss, took the full brunt of Chase's blow to the chin. There was a bone crunching sound as Max was lifted slightly off the ground from the blow. But he was tough, and as soon as he had regained his balance, he was swinging at Chase again—this time connecting square on his left cheek. There was a dazzling flash of light that exploded in front of Chase's eyes as the hit registered. Chase stumbled backwards, tasting the blood in his mouth. Then he smiled.

All the bottled up desperation, pain, longing, rage, and bitterness Chase had inside came howling to the surface in an instant. Chase relished the hit, the taste of blood in his mouth, the brief second of searing pain that rushed into his face—all the noise around him faded away. He no longer heard Miriam's desperate screaming, the traffic driving steadily along, or the yell of Max's friends—all his concentration was focused on Max.

Max stepped in to swing again, but this time Chase blocked his arm, taking a blow to his own arm in the process. Then he savagely grabbed onto Max's hair and brought his head thundering down into his knee, which was flying up in anticipation. Chase felt his opponent's eye squish inward at the impact. Max fell backwards onto the ground with a thud.

In the heat of it all, his senses heightened to new levels of awareness. He felt the slight shift in the breeze as it sifted by. He recognized all the cracks in the labyrinth of hot, black asphalt in the parking lot. He calculated the exact spot Max would land before he hit the ground, and most importantly, he gauged Max's two friends as they charged roaring wildly at him from both sides.

Chase was able to throw a fast jab into the nose of the first before he reached him, but he got tangled up with the other one as the guy grabbed his shirt, ripping it and throwing Chase to the ground. Chase hit hard, and felt the pavement scrape at his unprotected arms while bruising his knees. The one who had thrown him to the ground now swung his leg back in order to kick Chase square in the head, but Chase threw up his arms in protection, managing to hang onto the foot and throw the other off balance. Chase quickly got to his knees, but just as he looked up, he was greeted by a tightly packed fist to the eye. The blow stunned him, as he was knocked back down onto the pavement. The pain was startling, a hot white flash burning in his face. The pain only served to fuel Chase's fury. Suddenly he was being hauled to his feet by two rough sets of hands. Tweedle Dee and Tweedle Dum had him from both sides, and their fearless champion, Max, now bleeding profusely from the mouth, spat blood furiously as he approached Chase. He stuck Chase once in the stomach making him double up, and then in the face—knocking him over.

Chase lay on the ground, his body mulched and bloody, but a heightened sense of awareness still flowed throughout his body. As Max walked along next to Chase, thinking him knocked out, Chase struck with lightning agility, twisting Max's leg and pulling him down to the ground. Chase wrapped his arm around Max's neck, and with his own back on the ground, he squeezed with everything he had.

Chase had lost touch with reality—every primal instinct in his body told him to rip the life from his enemy's lungs. It was the apex of his blood rage, and had he held on just a few seconds longer, he would have crushed Max's windpipe. Then something happened to stop him.

Through the scarlet haze of his blurred vision, he saw Miriam's face above him. Terrified teardrops poured from her face as she screamed at Chase to let go. Seeing her so distraught snapped him back. Instantly the energy was gone from his limbs, and they flopped onto the pavement next to him. He stared up at the sky through clouded eyes, not knowing what to think. He was vaguely aware of Max rolling off of him and onto the pavement, gasping like a fish for air. Also, he became aware that people were rushing over. Miriam, after first glancing at Max, came and knelt down at Chase's side. She stared down at him, her eyes bright with fear and tears. She gently touched his face, and he recoiled, grimacing at the tenderness of his bruised face. He was helped to his feet by a man in a black suit, and Miriam soothingly guided him away toward the car. They did not wait around, but hopped straight into the car and quickly drove back to the house for painkillers and ice.

Chase stumbled into the house with Miriam's help, and plopped down on the couch. Miriam had called her mom on the way home, and Susan rushed over to check Chase out. His eye was beginning to swell; it resembled a plump purple grape. His cheek was scratched and beginning to swell, but his teeth were fine. Chase's red Foo Fighters shirt lay haggard and shredded on his sore frame. His shoulder and ribs were bruised to some extent, but remained the least of his worries. Bloody, dirty elbows rubbed against his sides. His knuckles were on fire as well, scratched and swelling with bloody flakes plastered on. He had overcome his initial daze form the car ride, and was busy trying to set Susan's mind at ease.

"I'm all right," Chase argued his eyes trying to focus. "I just need some painkillers and a little bit of ice for the swelling. Nothing's broken as far as I can tell."

"Oh honey! You just lie right there—I'll have you all fixed up in a jiff," Susan responded rushing off into the kitchen for first aid supplies.

Chase glanced over at Miriam who was sitting apprehensively nearby. He gave a feeble smile and started trying to apologize for his actions.

"No," Miriam replied. "Don't apologize, it wasn't your fault. You were just trying to stick up for me when that jerk swung at you. I'm just so sorry you had to go through that. I had no idea he'd go insane like that.

You're not in any trouble—just lie back and try to relax okay?"

"Yeah…but I was wrong too. I drew him out there," Chase admitted. "I hope you'll forgive me. I just got caught up in it, and I was mad that he treated you so badly…I guess I was almost hoping something would happen just so I had a chance to get back at him; that was wrong, and I'm sorry you had to see that. I hope you'll forgive me."

She sat staring at him, not knowing how to respond. Then she stood up, walked over to the couch, and sat down next to him. She leaned over and kissed him on the cheek. Chase looked up in surprise.

"I understand why you did it," she whispered in his ear. "No one has ever stuck up for me like that before…I—"

Just then her mother came fussily back into the room, loaded down with supplies, cutting Miriam off mid phrase. Miriam backed away, staring Chase full in the eyes, sharing something secret between them. Then Susan was standing over him pulling out hydrogen peroxide and dabbing cotton balls into it. Miriam left the room, and Chase's thoughts followed after her. It was short-lived daze; the sting of the peroxide on his open wounds brought him back into the moment.

"I thought you're trying to help me—not finish me off!" Chase yelped, trying to joke, although being somewhat serious too.

"It'll only sting for a second, but we need to do it to clean out the open cuts. I'm sorry dear, but if we don't you could end up in a lot more trouble than you are right now."

"Yeah I know," Chase acquiesced, "just be gentle with me." He fluttered his eye lashes at her.

Susan helped clean all his gashes and cuts, bandaging them up with the skill of a seasoned veteran. Chase was content to sit back and let the painkillers take effect as she finished bandaging his extremities. Finally, she gave him a bag of frozen peas to put over his cheek and eye. It stung like crazy at first, but then simmered down to a dull throbbing numbness. He had been sitting on the couch for about fifteen minutes when Lance walked through the door.

"Hi all," he greeted. "What the ... ?" he said, catching sight of Chase sprawled out on the couch with a bag of iced peas on his face.

"Max started a fight with him," Susan said coming into the room.

"What?" Lance bellowed out in surprise. "What happened? I want to know how this started."

Miriam, hearing her father, came into the room. She and her mother related what had happened, with Chase occasionally jumping in. When everything had been told, Lance stood there shaking his head.

"I can't believe Max would do something like that," he said. "He always seemed like such a nice kid when he would come around. I never had anything against him."

They all sat quietly letting these last few words drift slowly through the room and into nothingness. Lance looked up in the stillness that followed, as if seeing Chase for the first time.

"Almost forgot," he said, "I was able to pick up that part for you. You probably won't be able to help me put it on, though, but that's all right. I should be able to do most of it by myself, and whatever I need help with I'll get Miriam to pitch in a little. Is that all right with you?" he asked, glancing over at Miriam with quizzical eyes.

"Yeah, no problem," she responded. "Do you just want to get that done now? Or after dinner?"

"I can start tearing things apart right now, and then after dinner if you could help out for about twenty minutes or so, I think we can get it all set."

Lance faced Chase once again, and eyed him up and down.

"Shame," he muttered half to himself, half out loud, "never would have thought Max would do something like that..." His voice trailed off as he went out to the shop.

"How would you like to take a warm bath?" Susan asked Chase. "I can run some water, and you can wash off and just lie down and soak and relax. Does that sound good?"

Chase felt achy and grimy. He agreed to the suggestion. He continued to lie on the couch, feeling exhausted and starting to go numb, while Susan went in to start the bath water. Miriam came over and sat on the arm of the couch, looking down on him.

"So…does this mean you're leaving tomorrow?" she asked.

There was a hint of misery in her voice. Chase picked up the subtle longing in her tone, beckoning him to remain, to stay with her. He did not know how to respond, he was busy tasting the colors of drugged up insomnia.

"I don't know," Chase confessed, shaking off the haze. "Will you do something with me? It would mean the world to me. Meet me tonight at midnight on top of the barn. I just want to be with you tonight, in case this is our last night together."

"I'll be there," she agreed. "The stars should be amazing tonight."

"I know," he replied, "I want to share them with you."

Just then Susan walked into the room.

"Bath is all ready for you," she said.

Chase shakily got up, cringing at his stiffness. He hobbled toward the tub, focusing on just putting one foot in front of the other. When he was in the bathroom, he closed the door and stripped off his torn and filthy clothing. He stared at himself in the mirror for the first time since the fight. His right eye was purple and fruity, but the swelling had gone down thanks to the ice. His left cheek throbbed, but on the outside the signs of the scuffle failed to attract much visible attention. His elbows were scratched, his knees were yellow like a ripened pear, and his side was a mixture of blue and yellow and brown. *All in all, not too bad,* he reflected. *I really did get off fairly lucky ... and who would have thought I could actually beat that guy?*

Chase shook his head as he climbed into the tub. It stung at first, but was immediately followed by a comforting sensation. He lay back, nearly submerged, and relaxed his body and mind. Melancholy began to slowly leak in as he stared at his toes sticking up just above the surface.

Plummeting down ... nothing to stop me, he thought. *Miriam ... not always here. Contentment only in the company of others? It still ends with me. Soft orange circles rimming my eyes. Just let them swallow me whole ... melt away ... tepid nonexistence.*

A sensation on his left wrist teased his attention. He brought his arm up in order to examine the source of the flapping. A wet, skin colored Band-Aid, soggy and swollen, had partially peeled off his wrist and swayed in the water revealing a thin, precise slash running along his skin. Chase squinted at the incision trying to make sense of it. He lifted his other arm to discover that he had an identical, skin colored bandage stretched over that wrist as well. It was soggy, but clung grimly onto his body. He stared through sad eyes at them, and the half blurred, tired memory came back to him.

Loud music, laughter, red plastic cups floating in people's hands. Sometime late. Friend's house ... party.

It was after twelve. *How much have I had to drink?* Chase thought, swaying as he stared down at an empty bottle in his hand. People were all enjoying themselves. *Fine; let them. I wish I had a knife ...*

Chase stumbled upstairs, searching for a quiet place to sit. He had been excited for the party, the first one after graduation: a kick off to summer. The alcohol had sent him into suppressed feelings of loneliness though. He had sat downstairs, drinking, drinking, and trying to make himself disappear. Suicidal thoughts flirted. A blade: the euphoric sensation of pain and escape. The slow loss of consciousness, the departure ... these thoughts floated to life inside Chase's intoxicated brain.

Why not? Find a knife.

Chase stumbled into his friend's room, where he found a switchblade resting casually on the cluttered dresser top. Grabbing the blade, he collapsed heavily onto the floor, his back resting against his friend's bed.

There were no tears, no thoughts of family or friends, no feeling of satisfaction—just a numb acceptance. Random thoughts passed through his mind.

Skin... the blade slips easily down... slight pain... soon gone... am I floating? Just drip on my clothes, not Stephen's floor... second cut... black red... happy? No... nothing... never happy...

Chase closed his eyes waiting for the end. There was the sudden sound of a door opening.

"Chase? Chase!"

Light flooded the room. *There was a slamming sound. Energetic arms are shaking me. Eyelids flutter open. A mouth, nose, and dark wide eyes stare down. Stephen... it's Stephen.*

He may have saved my life then, Chase thought without emotion. *He was discreet about it. Bandaged me up right there in the room. Told me we were going to the hospital. I said no. It wasn't bad. Gave me a little food and water. Sat by me until I fell asleep. Probably just trying to cover himself; his parents were out of town.*

Chase shrugged, not caring much either way. Chafed and worn out, he lay stretched in the tub trying to relax. He put any coherent thoughts from his mind, and listened, ears submerged, to the innocuous silence of the warm bathwater. He was beginning to nod off when there was a knock on the door. Chase sat upright, listening to verify the legitimacy of the sound, and he heard it again, this time accompanied by a voice.

"Chase? Is everything all right?" The faint question drifted through the thinly paneled door.

"I'm just getting out," he replied. "Be there in a minute or two."

"All right, I brought you your bag with clean clothes in it. It's outside the door, so just wrap your towel around yourself and grab it when you get out."

"Thank you very much," he said. "I'll be out soon."

Chase spent the remainder of the evening masking his doubts and growing melancholy—the mask was beginning to fit his face better and better all the time. No one suspected anything lurking beneath his relaxed and courteous manner. After dinner Chase helped put the finishing touches on his car. It was now road ready.

"I really appreciate everything you guys have done for me," Chase said. "Thank you so much for your hospitality and help—I don't have very much money right now, but I'll pay you back for money you spent on parts for my car as soon as I get home again."

"Oh, don't even worry about it," Lance replied. "It was just the right thing to do; we don't want your money, but thanks for the sentiment."

"Besides," Susan chimed in, "we enjoyed having you around. It's been awhile since the boys have lived at home. It was nice."

"Anyway, thanks again," Chase said, almost blushing.

"You're welcome here anytime, hon," Susan responded. "You aren't leaving tonight are you?"

"No, but first thing tomorrow I'll be heading out. I think I'm going to call it a night—it's been a long couple of days."

"All right, well I'll be up in the morning to make you some breakfast—send you off on a good note," Susan stated.

"Oh, you don't have to …"

"Nonsense! Why, you'll probably sleep clear till noon again anyway," she said laughing.

They all laughed together at this. Chase got up then and started heading toward the guest room. He locked eyes with Miriam, and the unspoken agreement passed between them: outside, at the barn, midnight. Chase softly closed the door behind him.

He flopped down on the bed, exhausted and aching. Each breath made him cringe a bit from the bruising on his ribs. He closed his eyes, but could not sleep. His mind wouldn't let him. All he could think about was Miriam—Miriam and how even the amazing time spent with her could not erase the pain in his heart. Chase lay staring at the ceiling, lost in a sea of evanescent long-ings and wishes that evaporated all around him.

The minutes ticked by, and hours followed. Still he lay looking up out of eyes shrouded with uncertainty and doubt. Finally it was midnight. Chase knew what he had to do—he knew it before he got up and climbed out the window to meet Miriam. It would not be easy, but it was the only decent thing he could do. *Someday,* he thought, *things might be different.*

The two embraced outside. Miriam was wearing a blue sweater and carried a thick blanket in her arms. They carefully made their way to the top of the barn, where they sat close together, wrapped in the warm confines of the quilt. They leaned in on each other, not speaking, just being with one another. The hint of dark cloud began to form overhead.

Chase took her hand in his, her soft skin nestling against his.

"I'm going to miss you," she spoke suddenly, her words breaking the silence.

"I'll miss you too … I'll miss you a lot. But I'll come back. Soon hopefully … but I just don't know yet."

"I don't want this to come across as weird … but I feel like I've known you for so much longer," Miriam said. "Like I feel so natural around you, there's no fak-ing or awkwardness or any of that. I mean … what do you think?"

"No, totally, I feel the exact same way," he replied. "Being around you these last two days has been the best time I've had in long time. Just everything about you is amazing." Chase gave her hand a small squeeze as he spoke. "And I've never felt this way about any-one before…just everything about you, it's—you're so…you're beautiful."

Chase could feel the fire between them. She was so special. Her laugh, her smile, her genuineness, her soul—it was all beyond words.

They looked at each other then. She stared into his eyes, reading every unspoken thought that blos-somed there manifesting in the connection between them. She leaned in and kissed him then. It was short, but still managed to block out the world. It only made it so much harder to say what he needed to say. Their lips parted, and they stared through each other's eyes. Dark clouds had begun forming overhead, stealing the stars above. Then the rain began to fall.

They scrambled down from the rooftop, holding hands and dashing for shelter. When they reached the window to her room she beckoned him to join her, but Chase declined.

"I want to stay with you and just hold you—you know I do, but not now," he said. "I can't. It's just not the right time."

"I understand," she said, her eyes dropping. "Will you be here in the morning?"

"Yes," he replied, kissing her again as the raindrops fell. "Good-bye."

"Goodnight," she said, smiling back at him as he turned and retreated to his open window.

Chase climbed through the window and shut it behind him. He took off his wet clothing and put on some dry ones. Then he sat down heavily on the bed, his head in his hands.

He had lied to her.

Lying in his bed earlier that night he realized he had to go. There could be no waiting, or hoping for that fairy-tale ending of happily ever after. Chase could not pretend that being with her solved all his problems, that it gave him complete solace and triumph over the demons in his mind, or that it fulfilled his yearning for resolution. He loved her. He knew that was true. But he was drowning, and he would not allow himself to take her under with him. He loved her ... so he knew had to go. It could not end any other way—not now it couldn't—he had to leave.

Chase gathered his things, packed his bag, and retrieved the keys for his car. Then he sat down and wrote a note apologizing to Lance and Susan for his hasty departure, and promising to return on his way home to visit and repay them. He taped the note to the front of the guest room door. Finally, he wrote a short letter to Miriam, and slid it quietly under her door. Inside was written:

Miriam,

I said I would be here in the morning, but I can't be. I hope you will understand, and believe me when I say that it hurts me so much to leave without saying good-bye to you. I am not leaving forever, but I don't know when I'll be back. There are things in my life that are not all right. Every day is a fight just to get up and to keep going. You have been the best thing that has ever happened to me, but I can't be the person you deserve. Not now. I am torn inside and don't know how to change. At first I thought you were the answer to everything I was looking for, but I cannot be so naïve, especially at your expense. My problems lie with me, they always have, and I am the one who has to fix them. I won't drag you down with me. I do not know when I will see you again, because I do not know when I will find whatever it is I'm missing. I want you to know, though, that it was real—all of it. In my heart I know, beyond a doubt, that we shared something: something beautiful. I want you to know that I love you.

Chase

Chase did not hesitate for fear that he would not be able to leave. He used the window like before and hurried through the steady downpour toward his car. Hurriedly leaping inside, he turned the key. It fired to life, and he turned the wheel back and forth quickly to check its soundness. It reacted just fine.

The house faded away behind him as he slowly drove off. He thought of everything Lance and Susan had done for him, all their hospitality and care.

He thought of Miriam.

He thought of his flight.

And he watched the raindrops fall.

CHUCK

The rain melted over the windshield of Chase's Jeep as he drove through the darkness. It pelted the glass in droves, morphing into one cool, liquid sheet that was thrashed back and forth by the efforts of the windshield wipers. The headlights of the vehicle poked two small beams of yellow through the torrents of summer rain. Chase sat behind the wheel of the car with red-rimmed eyes, a tired mind, and a sleep deprived numbness to it all.

His mind wove tired thoughts through its receptors, uncaringly flushing them all away. The only thought that managed to elude the filters of his wasted brain was that of Miriam. Did he do the right thing? Why had he run? Was there really anything beyond what he had felt for her? Or was he going to drive faster and faster until he eventually just flew right into the sea?

I am nothing but a question mark in a period society, he thought. *And we all know there is no place for a question mark in a period society—oh, no, no, no. We must all fall in line, fall in line. Am I still on the road? Ha, ha kid, you left the road a long time ago...*

The rain was still plummeting from the sky. Visibility was low, and Chase stared out of milky eyes, as the car seemed to drive itself down the road, chasing the headlights in front of it. Each raindrop bounced off his skull as well as the windowpanes. It drummed on the panes. *I am a zombie... an astronaut... floating and watching the rain fall and the car steer itself.* This thought drifted from one side of his brain to the other without much interruption. *I am going to fall asleep at the wheel of this car. Shucks. I could pull over, but that would involve trying. Maybe the fireball would warm me up. Yeah. I would be marshmallow Chase, extra crispy, like the one that the little kid always leaves in the fire too long. Big, bubbly, broiling Chase. That would be—What the—*

Reacting with the quick speed of the moment, Chase wrenched the wheel to the left, managing to avoid the soaked, writhing creature on the soggy pavement. The small burst of adrenaline had managed to artificially shock his body into awareness. He slowed to a stop, pulling to the side of the road, and looked back in his rearview mirror. It was no use; he could see nothing through the black raindrops streaking down. Curiosity and adrenaline mixing through his system got the best of him, and grabbing a flashlight from the glove box, he hopped out into the cold downpour. The beam from the torch was feeble at best, and he squinted down its narrow shaft of light trying to identify the nightly apparition. There were no cars on the road, he had no memory of how long he had been driving for, but the sun was still far from rising—still very far away.

He heard it shrieking before the beam from his flashlight settled on the contorted creature. Its high pitched, agonized squeal sent liquid lightning down his spine. It was at once both completely alien and strangely human. It was horrific and painful. Reluctantly, Chase followed the source of the shrieking with the light clutched in his trembling hands. The beam settled on the source of the sickening lamentations.

The shape of a soaking, mangled dog met his eyes. Chase momentarily froze, shocked and ill at the sight of it. The dog appeared to be a yellow lab; it was not huge in size, and its coat of fur was soiled and grubby. The dog was desperately trying to drag its limp back half from the road and into the ditch. Its back legs were useless. They were twisted unnaturally, facing up at the sky. The dog's soft underbelly was ripped open revealing a slippery, dark, ruby-red protrusion of organs. The wretched creature cried out with each movement, and Chase was not sure if it was his lack of sleep or the rain, but it looked like big, salty tears ran down the dog's face.

The image was forever burned into Chase's memory. The initial shock wore off, and Chase hurried through the downpour to the dog's side. Chase's hair was plastered to his face, and the drops of water rushed over his face as he knelt down. The dog could not have been hit more than five minutes ago; it did not seem that it could have managed to stay alive much longer than that. Chase felt fury bubbling up inside of him as he thought of someone hitting the dog and then just driving off. He knelt next to the animal not knowing what to do and knowing there wasn't anything he really could do. The wounds were just as bad as he initially estimated, and warm, dark blood seeped out staining the pavement.

The first thought that ran through his head was to try and move the dog off the road and onto the softer grass bordering the ditch. However, he quickly realized any hope of moving the dog was completely fanatical. He sat there stunned and at a complete loss of what to do. The dog swiveled his head to look up at Chase. Its fur was soaked and muddy. Its cold, wet nose sucked air in quick, choppy bouts. And its tortured, innocent eyes stabbed Chase straight to the heart. They pleaded with him for an answer to this cruelty and suffering. They tried to understand why this was happening. Chase's heart seemed to collapse in on itself and plunge down into his stomach. He cradled the dog's head in his arm; the dog whimpered at his touch, but the fight was draining from its body.

"It's okay, baby. It's okay," Chase repeated over and over again as he clutched the dying animal in his arms.

He rocked gently back and forth, repeating, "It's okay, baby. It's okay," over and over. The rain fell all around on that dark strip of road, but Chase did not even realize he was outside anymore. His eyes were locked with the dog, sharing with it the last few seconds of its life. His words faded into whispers, then into nothing. The ineffable reality of death materialized in his mind. The dog stared up at Chase. It took one last strained breath, and then went limp. Chase watched as the life left its eyes. They glazed over, starting from the rims and closing in on the center in a dull shroud.

Chase continued feverishly rocking the dog's head back and forth in his arms, and his mind was suddenly in two different places.

The long hallway stretched ahead of him: plain, white, callous. Chase put one foot in front of the other—willing himself to make the trip. In the back of his mind, subconsciously, and faintly echoing was the fact that this would be the last Sunday he would ever be in this place. It amazed him how long that hallway was, yet when he reached the large, open door he felt as though he hadn't even walked there. The thought of fleeing crossed his mind. The usual crew of decrepit misfits sat in their wheelchairs nearby—slobbering and mumbling to themselves. Chase did not even remember having walked past them; his eyes had been focused on the end of the white tunnel, and his mind did not know what to think.

He was still standing just outside the doorway.

He hated that he didn't want to go in. He hated himself for his own selfishness. He hated that the last time he would ever see his grandfather would be like this.

Chase's grandfather had succumbed to cancer several months before, and throughout that time the family had visited once a week to this care center, which was merely a place to die; a place that was always too clean, too quiet, and too white. There was no fight in the place. It was a place where people came and watched the sallow walls and ceilings as who they once were withered away, just as their bodies also rotted and fell away. There was no dignity in such a place. Patients lay in their beds in excruciating pain or too drugged up to recognize their remaining time. They just lay there and waited to be no longer.

Chase hated this place. It was the tangible affirmation that his Grandfather was being stolen from him—robbed piece by painful piece. This once solid and remarkable man could now no longer even take a drink by himself. How was that all right? It made Chase crazy—feeling like vomiting and murdering at the same time.

Chase stood still in the doorway. Somehow, his legs began to move, and they carried him into the small, barren room. His parents stood next to the bed, trying to talk with the shrunken, pasty man that lay in his grandpa's bed. It was difficult to understand his grandfather much anymore; he had to fight through the coughing that wracked his frame as he choked on his own saliva. The effort reduced him to painful, barely audible whispers. After a couple short phrases, he would be breathing as if having just sprinted a mile. It hurt Chase to see him. It burned his heart.

The bones lay staring up at him as he walked over to the far side of the bed. Wrinkled flaps of gray skin hung loosely to the figure. Sunken, sad eyes looked up at him, trying so hard to be strong and appear all right for his grandson.

Chase knelt next to the bed and held his hand; it was cold and weak. The skin was still calloused and worn—proof of a long, well-used life. Chase knelt there and whispered a falsely encouraging greeting.

His grandfather's eyes watered. He spoke softly up to Chase, his voice cracking with emotion Chase had never witnessed before.

"You're a good boy, Chase," his voice choked. "You're a good kid..."

His voice trailed off as he stopped to catch a raspy breath. His eyes closed, and his face contorted as a small coughing spell seized his chest and throat. He fought for each breath that passed over his yellowing, worn-down teeth. It was too much for Chase to handle. He had to get out of there, but first he leaned over his Grandfather's forehead and kissed it. It was dry like a sun-baked leaf—dry and cold.

"I love you, Grandpa," he said giving his hand a squeeze.

Chase left then. He walked away without turning his head, leaving his parents to the remainder of their visit. He did not want to remember his Grandpa like that—no, he refused. He pushed the image out of his mind as fast as he could, seeking solace from the pain and hurt he was experiencing. He bitterly built a wall in his heart.

The rain poured savagely down from the heartless sky. It soaked Chase all the way to the marrow. He stared up at the firmament, the water beat his face like tiny slippery fists, and he screamed up at it all until his lungs gave out. Then the floodgates shattered behind his eyes, and he wept what felt like tears of blood. He choked on his own sobs as his body gave out, collapsing onto the pavement. He cried and cried. Every bottled up and repressed memory fueled his attack on the world. The tears stormed down his cheeks, and Chase laid on the ground and let it all happen.

Curled up on the ground bawling, Chase had no idea how long he remained there. The rain was beginning to let up, though, and the first hints of sunlight peaked over the ridges. Chase was near complete exhaustion, eyes staring out at nothing, eyes with nothing left to shed. He became aware that he was shivering. He remembered the dog next to him, and forced himself to sit up. Its lifeless body sprawled next to him. Chase glanced down and noticed a green metal tag hanging from its collar. He took the tag in his hand and flipped it over to read the inscription. *Chuck.* The dog's name was Chuck.

Chase barely managed to hold back another wave of tears that welled up behind his eyes. He breathed deeply, closing his eyes and trying to focus. His hands were shaking. They were purple-blue and curved like claws in the cold. It was an effort to open and close his hands. Chase again looked down at the tag and finished reading.

Chuck's address was inscribed on the small, green piece of metal. Looking up, Chase realized that there was a driveway less than a hundred feet away. He got to his feet and stumbled closer to check the address in order to find out just where he was. The rain had altered to a steady misting. It was a cold, half-wet world that Chase waded through.

The address became legible. Chase shook his head, doing a double-take. It was the same address as on the tag. Chuck had been lacerated less than a hundred feet from his house.

Chase stood there at the end of the long driveway looking up at the dark, sleeping house. He sat there wondering what to do. He feared waking that slumbering house, which sprawled in the shadows before him. He turned, thinking to just leave and let the owners find their pet for themselves in the morning. *After all,* he tried to reason, *it wasn't me who hit the dog. They probably would not even believe me if I said I didn't do it.* He turned and started walking back to the Jeep. However, he was not careful enough, and his gaze fell on Chuck.

It was not right.

Chase knew in his heart that leaving like this was wrong, that he would be no better than the person who had hit Chuck in the first place. *Why though?* he thought. *There is no reason I should feel guilty for leaving... but it's Chuck. I can't leave like this. It's not my fault, but now it's my responsibility. I'm not going to be like that other person,* he thought fuming. *It's just plain wrong.*

The sky was beginning to brighten, as he stood surrounded in the wet haze. Chase found that he could make out the edges and borders of trees and fences much more clearly now. Dawn was rising, and with it rose the verification that everything that had happened to him those past few hours was real. His legs buckled under him, and he sat down hard on the coal-colored road. *Wow I'm tired,* he thought. His whole body hurt. His head refused to think anymore. His vision was blurred, and he did not know if it was him or just the mist all around him. His head turned, taking in aspects of his surroundings that jumped out at him, before forgetting them in the next second.

"I have to do it. I have to go tell them."

With an effort Chase pushed himself up off the road. Taking an instant to steady himself, like a drunk faking sobriety, he bid his legs carry him the distance. Utilizing the full power of his remaining thinking ability, Chase rung the small, circular, plastic dome of a doorbell, and waited for a response. Hearing nothing, he rang again ... and again. The soft scuffling of slippered feet on carpet could be heard within, as a light went on inside.

The door cracked open. Two beady, black eyes stared peevishly out. They squinted at Chase, seeking an explanation for this unusual visit. Chase stared at those dark, quizzical jellyrolls and almost let a giggle out. Then the tiny cave of a mouth opened, revealing an ordinary tongue and teeth. It spurted out a gruff phrase.

"Is there something you want?"

Chase stood there, emotionally drained, exhausted to the core, forgetting why he was there. Then he remembered. *Chuck. I'm here for Chuck.*

"Well?" the brusque voice asked, hinting at its annoyance.

"I'm sorry to bother you at this time, but there is a dog out on the road that's been hit, and I think it's yours."

The eyes were taken aback at this, but the shock was soon replaced with an accusatory glare. The eyebrows were suddenly pulled down to join the eyes in their vindictive stare.

"What? How do you know it's my dog? Did you hit it? Was it you?"

Chase was not surprised by this charge. He had expected it before he had even raised his hand to knock on the door. Still, he found himself unsure of how to respond. The fact that this man could stand there on the other side of small wooden door and blame him for the dog's death made his blood start to boil. *This guy didn't care for Chuck—he didn't* know *him. It is* his *fault the dog is dead, not mine,*" Chase thought. *I knew Chuck better in the five minutes I spent with him than this guy ever did.* Chase fumed. He was about to just turn and walk off when there was another voice resonating through the half cracked doorway.

"Dear, who is it?" the voice asked.

It was a woman, probably beady-eyes' wife. Something in that voice made him stop. It was more than just pleasant, it was caring. This voice was who Chuck belonged to. Chase opened his mouth to speak, but beady-eyes cut him off.

"It's about Chuck," he said. "This young man said he was hit by a car ... "

Before the man could go on any further, the door swung open and both voices were given substance and form. The man was roughly Chase's height, but held a good fifty-pound advantage over Chase. He wore a blue-striped bathrobe and matching slippers. He had an early morning beard, and a severe case of bed head. The woman was striking. She wore only pajama pants and an over sized T-shirt. Her hair was unkempt, and her face was not hidden behind a shroud of make up. All that being said, she glowed regardless. She was no model, but something beyond and outside of all that flowed about her. Chase was put at ease in her presence.

"What?" she gasped. "Is he all right?"

"I'm sorry," Chase responded, "but he's dead. I saw him lying in the street when I was driving, and pulled over to see if he was all right. There was nothing I could do. He died right after I arrived there ... I'm so sorry."

The woman began to cry, leaning against her husband who comforted her as best he could. Chase stood there saying nothing. It was an awful moment.

There was nothing more left to say. Chase turned and walked back to his car. As he was leaving he saw the couple standing over their deceased pet.

"Bye, Chuck," Chase whispered as he stared in the rearview mirror. "Bye..."

Chase's body felt like it had participated in a twenty-four hour rodeo and it had lost. His arms felt like dead weight, and his legs would barely work the pedals. He drove on for a couple miles before almost falling asleep at the wheel. He could go no further. He pulled over on the side of the road, fell into the back seat, buried his head between the seat cushions, and lost all consciousness.

Journal
June 21, 2009

If you value your time you should stop reading now. There is nothing of worth in anything I have to say. I sit alone on the top of this parking garage staring out across the lights and shapes. I have nowhere better to be, because there is nowhere worth being for any period of time.

> "I've got a gun in my hand but the gun won't cock,
> My fingers on the trigger but the trigger seems stuck,
> I keep on staring at the tick tock clock,
> But even if I could I would never give up"
>
>   -The Streetlight Manifesto

There is no gun in my hand; the bullet is already in my gut—its cold despair seeping through my veins.

I am the only person here. It's funny really, come on laugh with me: Ha ha!

I am in the wasteland!

T.S. Eliot has written my soul. I am in the wasteland, and it is my mind...wasting away in ludicrous indifference to it all. I read "The Catcher in the Rye" recently. I read it all in one night. It was superbly funny when Holden continues asking where the ducks go when the pond freezes over. I understand why that book is so revered. Really I do.

I was longboarding late the other night, and I happened to pass a church (Catholic, I'm pretty sure). I decided to go inside and see what God was up to. I walked to the doors and found they were locked. I guess he was out for the night. Along the side of the building there was a statue of one of the saints or someone and a kneeling stool with a light shining down upon it. I thought it was nice that I could leave a message for the Big Guy...whenever he got around to it. The batteries must be broken on his machine, though, 'cause I never hear anything from him." Father why have you forsaken me?" and all that. Whatever.

As I was boarding here tonight, I stayed on the left side of the road facing traffic for a lot of the trip. As each car would rush past, I would picture myself being hit by each of the various vehicles. The bus would pancake me. The motorcyclist and I would tango to the crunching of our bones. The mustang would flip me over the windshield before I splitter-splattered on the pavement.

> "The experience of each new age requires a new confession, and the world seems always waiting for its poet."
> —Ralph Waldo Emerson

Well I'm no poet, and my words are cheap. Will they all fall off the paper if I tip it up? Probably should. Let the wind carry off my words like leaves in the fall.

I was on ecstasy the other night—heroin-based ecstasy as opposed to speed-based ecstasy. I hear people die from that stuff occasionally. So it goes, eh Vonnegut? The X didn't kick in for a while. I smoked some weed and drank some alcohol while I waited. I think the only way to describe the sensation when it finally took over is to say it felt like I had injected pure rainbow into my system. Everything felt right, and everything meant something. That's ridiculous though, it's just the chemicals screwing with your mind and body—significant...ha, ha. I don't know why people are so wary of drugs though.

Coke, Mary Jane, Ecstasy, Crack, Heroin, Shrooms, LSD...

I'd do any and all of them if I had them around. And if not, I wouldn't. I just don't care. Uh oh—letting the Nihilist out of the cage! Ha, ha.

"Destruction is the creation of the youth." I wrote that in an English paper not long ago, and it has been on my mind recently. I think I got that idea from some of Camus' writings about the Absurd Man. The creation of a thing, that is, the giving an artistic median to the voice of the soul, that seems to be one of the highest aims of man. Why though? Why do we create? Fullfillment? Meaning? Justification of one's existence?

I am not creative. I am weak, pathetic, and petty. I struggle but create not. I battle but utter nothing significant. I scream at the Top Of My Lungs!!!!! But the noise dies having never been noticed.

I have no real ambition. I don't have motivation or a reason to try, because the things I wish for will never appear.

What is a soul mate? A soul mate is something I'll never have,' cause my wretched soul spits venom at anyone who comes too close. I'm desperately alone, but I can't help pushing people away...but maybe that's the one decent thing I could do for them. I may be sinking, but I've resigned to the fact that I'm going down alone.

I was talking to a former friend a while back, and throughout our conversation on drinking, which was merely her self-righteous tirade on how "drinking is dumb, and I'm so much better than everyone cause I deal with my problems without drinking and blah blah blah," she brought up the fact that people are so stupid,' cause they are taking shots of hard liquor, and they're not even enjoying it."

I don't want anyone to ever try telling me that drinking is just an escape.

I already know that!!! Why else would I do it? You don't know me or care about me. People like that really don't. And there are lots of them out there.

As I rode the other night I saw a catfish slipping through the dirty canal water down below. I stopped and stared at that jolly plump cat warbling through his dirty wet world. He avoided the shadows as if afraid of the night. I stood there sadly and prayed for the light.

I tried to kill myself the other night. Drinking did nothing to alleviate my mind that night. All I could think of was sitting on the floor of in a dark room staring up some blank ceiling with two silver, sharp cuts along my wrists and the warm living milk bubbling out my veins and me losing consciousness as I drifted away. He stopped me though. Some other time perhaps. Even though I cut myself, I doubt I would have died. The reason I cut my wrists is because, as I said before, I'm a coward, and the thought of jumping to my death terrifies me. I really don't fear death itself, and I guess somewhere inside I still possess the hope of something else, cause somehow I'm still here.

" And when we fall, we will fall together
No one will catch us, so we'll catch ourselves and when we run, we will run forever
no one will understand, what we meant."

　　　　　　　　　　 -The Streetlight Manifesto

I am falling with no one to catch me. Super.

" Turn in the door once and turn once only
We think of the key, each in his prison
Thinking of a key, each confirms a prison."

　　　　　　　　　 -T.S. Eliot, " The Wasteland"

Hopefully, for your sake, you never read this or got this far.

I puke gravel from my guts
and it spews on the page,
My spleen bursts on the ruts
And it burns a purple rage.

Screw thinking, be stupid. You'll be much
happier in the long run.

Just pray for an accident
and we'll all get to heaven

Enough of this, time to put on a mask
that still seems to care. Fake that illusion
just a little longer, Chase, my boy. Good
night one and all—wake me up when the world
is different.

DAVID

Chase rolled onto his side and squinted out the window. The sun was just coming up ... or down. Chase let his head fall once again onto the seat cushion, exhaling warm, stagnate air. *The sun is up,* he thought. *Tight ... another day.*

Where am I? What time is it?

Sitting up he felt every hit from his fight with Max resonate through his body. He winced at the stiff jolt.

"I need a cigarette."

Chase reached up and turned the key halfway on to see what time it was. The digital clock glowed to life. 8:13 a.m. He stared at the clock trying to make sense of the numbers. *What time did I fall asleep? Early in the morning,* he thought. *Did I really only sleep two or three hours? Unless ...*

Then it hit him: he had slept all day and night.

He groaned audibly. Rather then feeling refreshed and reenergized, he felt as if the sandman had pummeled him over the head. His joints were stiff and unresponsive, and his muscles felt strained and raw. *Way too much sleep,* he thought, rubbing his eyes. *Where are my Camels?*

Straining, Chase reached up front and grabbed his pack from its roost in the glove box. He tumbled out the door and stood stretching on the gravel. His arms tightened as they grabbed for the baby blue sky, his legs straightened till he stood tiptoed, and his mouth stretched cavernously in a greedy yawn.

Chase reached into his cigarette packet and pulled out one of the few remaining smokes he had left. Lighting it, he inhaled deeply, instantly feeling better as the smoke caressed his senses. Chase exhaled a cloud of temporal, ocean-gray smoke, glancing around to take in his surroundings. The sun was rising in the distance as the world lulled lazily around. There were short, coloring trees nearby, and soft, sloping grassy hills rolling off the horizon. A faded green car whipped by on the two-lane country road. Several houses sprawled among hickory trees and sparrow nests. They were plain houses, real houses: houses where people lived and worked and loved. Chase lit another cigarette, slowing down, relishing it. The sky yielded few clouds, preferring its own soothing blue canvas. It was still chilly outside from the previous night, but Chase enjoyed the shivers that prickled his skin and made tiny hairs stand up on his bare arms. He threw the butt of his cigarette down, rubbing its smoldering embers out with the sole of his Converse.

It hit then, creeping up, whispering in his ear, and crawling into Chase's brain. He felt lonely, desperately lonely. He wanted to be home. He wanted his family around. He wanted to talk to someone, anyone from back home. He missed his bed, and his shower, and his room, and his shelf full of depressing, old books. He needed a friend.

Kurt.

He wanted to talk to Kurt.

Chase fumbled in his jeans' pockets before remembering he had left his cell phone at home.

"Damn," he whispered under his breath. "Where can I find a phone?"

Staring down the road Chase saw no solution in sight. He immediately felt glum. His shoulders shrugged forward and his head drooped. *If I fell off the edge of the earth right now,* he thought, *would anyone even realize it?* Chase sat down hard, leaning up against the rough black leather of his Jeep's front tire, and stared out at the world through melting eyes. *What have I gained from this stupid trip?* he wondered bitterly. *Just a better reason to roll over and quit; that is all I have. Except for Miriam. But I ran. Why do I always do that? I royally sabotaged that one. I'm done. Enough is enough. I'm turning around and driving home ... or into some river ... whichever presents itself first, I guess.*

Chase stepped into the car, plopping down in low spirits, he started the engine. The gaslight flickered on with the rest of the car.

"Awesome. Freaking awesome," he spat, banging his hands on the wheel.

Where can I go to fill up? he wondered. Chase did not remember passing any place coming from Miriam's house, but he could have easily missed seeing any in the dark and the rain. Hesitating, he turned westward and continued running away from it all. There was no sign of a gas station. Brooding on dark thoughts and lonely memories, he drove on.

Several short minutes later he was rewarded with a sign announcing the upcoming town of Trimmons: population ninety-five. The town was only four miles up the way, and Chase coaxed his thirsty car on. It was nearing ten in the morning by the time Chase pulled into the meager excuse for a town. At first glance, it seemed the place had only one real road running through the middle of the various small buildings, and upon further examination, the initial estimate was proven correct. The town was comprised of one main strip.

Slowly rolling between the buildings, Chase felt something was amiss. The place was barren. There were no people out walking on the sidewalks, no shops bustling with customers, and not so much as a car sitting parked on the street. Everything appeared to be shut down. A small two-pump gas station caught his eye, and he veered into the lot. It was closed. There was a sign on the door, and Chase hopped out of the car to see what it said. "Closed for Church" was written in big block letters on the sign. "Back at eleven-thirty." *So it is Sunday,* he pondered. *I did sleep that long after all. Dang.*

As Chase glanced around, he spotted a rundown pay phone along the side of the gas station. The booth appeared neglected—a small piece of a bygone era. Its blue paint was weather worn and stripping, but all complaints aside, when Chase picked up the receiver and dropped in two quarters the steady hum of a dial tone reverberated into his eardrum. Hopes raised, he dialed Kurt's number from memory. It rang four times without an answer. Then the groggy sound of his friend's voice:

"Hello?"

"Hey man," Chase said. "Just wake up?"

"Chase?" The voice perked up. "Is that you?"

"Yeah, man. It's me."

"Chase! Dude, what the hell? Where are you? What's going on? I tried getting a hold of you the other day, and your parents told me you were gone. Are you all right?"

"Whoa, slow down buddy, one at a time. I'm all right; I just needed to hear a friendly voice. That's all."

"Uh, yeah. Well thanks," Kurt replied. "You worried the hell outta me, man. Not cool. Now really, what's going on? 'Cause I know you, and honestly, I'm a little freaked out right now."

"Yeah, I'm not going to bother lying. I'm having a bit of a tough time right now—but don't worry, I'll be heading home soon."

I hope, he thought.

As they were talking, Chase looked around the town. *Old buildings mostly—not even a McDonald's here,* he thought. Then he noticed a parking lot filled with cars, and it caught his attention. It was the parking lot for a church. The church was a simple wooden structure. Nothing in its physical appearance jumped out at Chase as being in any way significant. It humbly sat with its parking lot of cars wrapping along its side.

"Chase, are you there?" Kurt spoke, his voice rising through the mouthpiece.

"Yeah—yeah, sorry," Chase apologized. "I was just looking around this little town I'm in. Small place. What'd you say?"

"I asked where you are and when you're coming home. What have you been *doing* these last few days?"

Suddenly talking to Kurt made him sad for no reason at all. He was so blue he wanted to die right then and there. What was he thinking calling him? Chase had nothing to say to his friend. There wasn't a person in the world he felt he could talk to. He had made a terrible decision. The muffled words on the other end seemed to slow down into a warm humming. Chase stared around him, turning slowly. He forgot he was still on the phone.

Chase shook his head, rubbing the haze from his eyes. He could still hear Kurt's voice on the phone. Without pausing to hear what he was saying, he spoke without tone into the black mouthpiece.

"I'm sorry. I have to go. I'll call again when I get the chance. I'm fine man, don't worry. Good-bye."

With that he hung up and sat down on the cement curb. His head hung, gazing down between his legs. He stared at the char-black pavement. *This must be how zombies feel. I am a zombie on too many prescription drugs without enough loving hugs. Ha ha, I am a zombie poet. I am William Corpseworth.*

He laughed out loud to himself. "Oh boy…I should just go find a nice, quiet place and commit myself. Lock me up and throw away the key. Don't let that one out—oh no, not him: he's not right in the head!"

Looking up then, Chase set eyes once again on the church. A cold stare came over his face, with his eyes hardening.

"Come on, man. You've avoided it every time I've brought it up, and I know you aren't busy this next

Tuesday night, 'cause I heard you talking in class. So, how about it? Come to youth group with me?"

"All right, if nothing else comes up before then, I'll go."

"Right on," Ronnie said with a grin. "I'll catch ya later."

It was Chase's junior year of high school, and for the past few weeks, Ronnie had brought up going to youth group. Ronnie did not run in the same circles as Chase, but they were acquaintances and had been paired up in class before on group projects. Chase tried not to let on, but he was actually interested in finding out what youth group was all about. Not today, though—today was Friday, and school was getting out for the weekend.

At home later that evening Chase got a call from Kurt.

"Hey man, get dressed. We're going to Sam's tonight. His parents are away, so he's throwing a big party or something."

"Uh, I don't know. I'm pretty tired . . ."

"Yeah, yeah, and you'd rather go to bed at 9:00 p.m. on a Friday night," Kurt mocked. "We'll take my car. I'll be by at like 9:30. Later!"

Chase hung up the phone, staring at nothing in particular. *Well,* he thought, *guess I'm heading out tonight. Now where did I leave my Camels?*

At almost 9:30 exactly, there was a knock on the door, and Chase scrambled down the stairs to get it, yelling behind him as he went:

"I'm going to Kurt's! Be home tomorrow sometime!"

Not sticking around to hear a response, he trotted out the door, and they both hopped into Kurt's Mustang. They took their time driving, and when they pulled into the street Sam lived on, they had to park several houses down, because plenty of other cars already lined the sidewalks. The party was well underway.

It was cold outside, even for early November. They walked briskly together toward the house, hands tucked in pockets and arms tight against their sides. As they walked up toward the front door, they saw Sam standing in the doorway ushering several people inside who were standing around smoking.

"Come on, guys. We need everyone inside or out back. No one can stand out here or else the cops are going to get called," he said, waving people inside.

Chase did not know Sam well, but Kurt did. He simply nodded at him as they entered, and let Kurt do the talking. It was warm inside, and the place was already packed. Chase saw a few friends from school and walked over. They all stood around talking and joking amongst themselves. Then, looking across the room, Chase could barely believe what he was seeing.

Coming through the door way was Ronnie. In one hand he held a dark bottle, and clutched in his other hand was a half-smoked joint. *What in the world...?* Chase thought, standing in a confused stupor. Ronnie was making a bit of a scene, but everyone seemed to love it. He was drinking, laughing, smoking, and bumping into several girls nearby—he was a one-man show. Chase couldn't help laughing at the irony of it.

"What's so funny?" his friends asked.

"Ha ha, oh nothing," Chase replied. "See that kid over there? Yeah, him—he invited me to go to youth group with him next week. So either God's out for the night, or Ronnie's his favorite," Chase finished laughing.

"Ha ha ha—yeah, I guess as long as you pray enough God doesn't care what you do on Friday night."

"Ha! That's really how it is, though. Christians are no different than us. The only difference is, they tell everyone to follow God and then they don't. We just skip the whole phony religion stuff to begin with," Kurt laughed. "Hypocrites."

They all laughed together, but Chase felt something sink inside him.

Ronnie is no different, he thought. *No one is. Everyone is just caught up in a mad whirlwind, and some people need religion to hobble along with. All gods and idols make no difference in the long run, and that is because when it comes down to it we are alone—completely alone. All we*

have is a floating ball in space populated by selfish inhabitants. The world spins round and round into Chaos. We all
begin, and end, and go so unnoticed and unremembered. In
the end everyone winds up dead—the good, the bad, and
the religious—it makes no difference how you get there.

Chase sat staring. His hand reached into his pocket
and dug around for a cigarette, but came up with an
empty packet. *Crap,* he thought, *and everything in this
stupid town is closed. No gas and no nicotine—just church.
There is nothing I can do but wait.*

A crazy idea entered his head then, and he could
not shake it. It was compelling and urgent. When he
tried to brush it aside, it returned stronger than before.
"Go see what's going on in there," it seemed to whisper in his ear. "Why not?" it argued. "You'll only be
sitting out here for another hour, why not go see what's
so exciting? Do you really have *anything* left to lose at
this point?" Chase laughed out loud at this thought.

"Well," he said to himself, "here goes nothing."

Chase strolled across the street and walked into the
parking lot. As he was heading past one of the parked
cars, he caught a fleeting reflection of himself on the
glass. The apparition Chase glimpsed startled him so
much that he stopped outright and peered at the mirrored surface of the glass. The swelling on his face had
increased since the fight, and his bruised eye was more

apparent than ever. It looked like he had been fighting, and it appeared that he had not been the victor. The skin surrounding his eye was a deep purple and black. The side of his lip had swollen, throwing his face off balance and doing a remarkable job of making him look silly. Chase had to laugh at his own reflection; there was really nothing else to do. Bringing his hands up, he primped his hair jestfully. Then, with a blown-up air of pompous and dignified importance, he marched zanily toward the double-door entrance like a proud old hobo in rags and tatters.

Once he reached the door, he grew more cautious and sought to open the doors as noiselessly as possible. He slipped through the doorway without so much as a sound, but the doors clattered behind him. Every head in the congregation swiveled around to eye the latecomer. Chase did not pause to let them gawk, but walked to the closest row in the back and sat down unperturbed. Everyone turned their attention back up front.

Settling in after the initial clumsiness, Chase set his attention on the man up front. The pastor was an older black man in his late fifties or early sixties, Chase guessed, with gray hair slowly turning a fleecy white. He spoke with authority, though, and passion that easily rivaled men half his age. And his eyes burned with life.

The presence this man resonated on stage amazed Chase. There was nothing especially unique about him physically, but when he spoke, Chase felt drawn in by the power of his words. He began to listen to this fiery old man's message. The sermon he was preaching was on Noah and the flood, but what he was drawing from this seemingly basic children's story impressed Chase. Never had Chase been exposed to anything beyond the mere tale of the animals going into the ark two by two, so he sat and listened with interest at this stranger's interpretation.

"And did God destroy the inhabitants of the earth in wrathful spite? Was it merely a hateful act on His part? Of course not! For God is a God of mercy and love! As it says in John 3:16, 'For God so *loved* the world that he gave his only begotten son, that whosoever believes in him shall not perish, but have ever lasting life.' This is no cosmic sadist! So how then could God allow all those people to perish in the flood? If God truly is omnipotent, then why did he not save every single person from that great deluge? The Creator of the heavens and earth did not take it upon himself to save everyone, because they had the choice all along to repent, and sadly they chose not to. Noah did not build the ark overnight—it took years. And where were the inhabitants of the earth when Noah warned them of the impending doom? They were there. They were mocking him.

"Mankind has the gift of free will. However, when they first sinned against God in the garden of Eden, they were endowed with the knowledge of good and evil. Why would God let this happen? He let it happen because without choice, without free will, His ultimate goal of having fellowship with His creation would cease to be of any worth. Mankind was created blameless—they were not created with any blame against them, for how could a perfect God create sin? They were created sinless, for how could He create anything against his own nature? But they were not created *faultless,* and that is how man had the capacity to choose, and when man rebelled against God, he brought the curse down upon himself. Mankind has to have the ability to choose God, or else they would simply be robots following preprogrammed responses. The only way to allow humanity to choose Him was to give them the choice between Him and an alternative. With the fall of mankind into sin began the slow process of God mercifully and patiently trying to bring us back to Him. The flood is a divine act of mercy and intervention on His part."

The preacher paused there and stared out across the audience. Chase was intrigued by the sermon as he slouched nonchalantly in the back. *It's an interesting idea anyway,* he thought. *It could make sense ... but so could evolution.* Regardless, his curiosity was piqued, and he listened reflectively to the stranger's words.

"How is the flood, the killing off of almost the entirety of humanity, an act of mercy, you ask. It is an act of mercy, because if God had not intervened when he had, any hope of mankind's salvation and redemption through His ultimate plan would have died with Noah. Noah was the *only* righteous man alive. And it was by God's grace that mankind was given a second chance through the purging of the flood. This was not the only time God had to directly intervene, however, as the tower of Babel is another example. By God stepping in and confusing their tongues He helped them avoid the willful collaboration of their prideful hearts. This, like the flood, was a mercy designed to postpone the end of humanity until He had a chance to bring Christ into the world, to bridge the gap between a Holy God and a mob of undeserving, rebellious creatures. God is a God of love and mercy, for only the Infinite has the ability to make Itself known to the finite, and that is exactly what God has done through the Bible, and through his Son.

"One last thought I'd like to leave you all with before you go is that the flood is a tremendous symbol of the heart of man, the justice, wisdom, and mercy of God, and that the work is not yet accomplished. The heart of man is bent toward doing what is wrong, and only God can open the heart's eye to His truth. The glory is God's, for He is always seeking to reveal Himself to us, and only through His condescension to our level can we then have the ability to ask forgiveness for our own glaring inadequacies. Human nature is not yet transformed into God's nature, but He is continuing His work, and we have His unfailing promise that He is with us always, even till the end of the age. What a blessed promise that is. Let us pray."

Everyone bowed their heads as the preacher said a prayer. Chase sat looking out over their heads, staring up at the preacher behind his meager, wooden pulpit. His initial awe by the pastor's words and charisma was being replaced with an air of cynical skepticism. *Sure anyone can make something sound legitimate with well-employed pathos, but that doesn't make it true—not in the least. Still… what if there is something to it?* Chase considered. *What if the biggest secret ever pondered was no real secret at all… and it has always been hidden right there, in plain sight, right under my nose? Could this honestly be the purloined letter of humanity? I have to talk to this pastor—I need to understand more.*

People were standing and huddling together in groups now that the service was over. An elderly couple sitting in the row in front of Chase turned around to greet him. They were poised and polite, staring at him without seeming to judge his uncouth appearance.

"Are you just passing through?" the elderly gentleman asked.

"Yes," Chase replied. "I'm on my way to Portland to see some relatives. The pastor up there, what's his name?"

"Oh," the lady answered, "that's Pastor David. Isn't he something? A very intelligent and caring man—would you like to meet him?"

Seeing that this was as good a chance as any to introduce himself to the pastor, Chase agreed. He followed the couple as they wound their way through the small circles and scattered individuals. They walked in single file, like an eel gliding through the water, sometimes brushing up against people as they squeezed through. The pastor was talking with someone as they walked up, but noticing them standing by, he turned and smiled warmly.

"Michael, Judith, always a pleasure," he said shaking their hands.

The pastor then extended his hand toward Chase, who stood by.

"Hello, I'm David."

"I'm Chase. Sorry about interrupting when I came in, I didn't realize how loud those doors were."

"Oh, no problem at all. We're glad you could make it. Are you visiting someone here?"

"Passing through actually," he replied. "I stopped for gas, but they were closed. So I thought I'd see what was going on over here while I waited. I'm not exactly a regular church attendee, but I thought your message was interesting."

"Well I'm glad you stopped in. We're more than happy to have you. Say," David continued, "do you have anywhere to eat lunch? If not, my wife and I would love to have you over. I don't know what your schedule is like, but you're more than welcome to eat with us."

"Uh, well I don't want to impose or anything ... "

"Oh, it's no imposition at all," David chimed in. "Most Sundays we have someone over at the house to visit. I understand if you're not really comfortable, and that's fine too. I won't be offended. The offer stands, though—if you're interested."

"Well, actually, I am running low on money," Chase admitted, blushing. "So if you're sure it wouldn't be a problem ... "

"You're more than welcome," David assured. "Just let me inform the Mrs. here real quick, and we'll be leaving in a little bit."

"Thanks a lot," Chase said. "That's really nice of you."

Inside, Chase was pleased. *Hopefully I'll get a chance to just talk with this guy one-on-one,* he thought. *I might even learn something! Doubtful. But who knows. Religion might not be so bad,* he mused, *if it weren't for people ... or hell for everyone who isn't good enough ... or if God was really there.*

Chase stood off by himself, not feeling like engaging in cheap conversation with people he would never see again. He stood waiting alone for the pastor and his wife to finish their socializing. After most people had filed out, the pastor and his wife made their way over to him, and together they all exited.

"Would you like a ride?" the pastor's wife inquired. "I'm Linda, by the way."

She smiled a full smile at Chase, extending a delicate hand. She had a warm, almond-colored skin and deep, auburn eyes. She was much shorter than Chase and looked to weigh no more than a hundred and fifteen pounds. She had the aura of a seasoned mother about her, and the warmth she radiated drew Chase in. He immediately felt at ease around her.

"Chase," he replied as he gently shook her hand. "Thank you, but I'll just follow in my car. Your husband said it was only a little ways off. My car is parked right over at the gas station. So I'll run over and grab it real quick, and then I'll be ready."

"That sounds fine," she said. "There's no rush. We'll be right here when you get back."

Chase jogged across the street to his car and climbed inside. He considered getting gas before he drove back across, but thinking it a bit rude, he decided against it. Realizing once again the clothes he was in, he felt his face flush and made a mental note to change when he got to David and Linda's house. Chase went to stick the key in the ignition, only to have it jam on him. Finally, he found the sweet spot. The key slid innocently in like nothing had happened. So with a swear, a twist, and a flare, the engine revved to life— sputtering in the noontime stillness.

The pastor and his wife lived only a short distance from the church in a small but suitable home. Chase was shown around and treated like a guest of honor. Lunch was prepared, and although Chase was famished, he controlled his appetite. It was a very satisfying meal of venison stew and fresh baked biscuits on the side. Chase was encouraged by his hosts to extra helpings of the stew, which he accepted. The meat had been cooking for several hours and nearly melted in Chase's mouth. Over the course of the meal, they made small talk together. Chase learned that David and Linda had lived in this small town for just over ten years and that they had three children who had all grown up and moved on. They told him how they had first come to this place and their pleasure in living away from cities and noise and pollution.

Chase, in return, told snippets about himself and his family. The atmosphere in the room was very much relaxed and only tensed once when Linda tentatively brought up the bruising on Chase's face. He thought quickly on the spot, fabricating a tale of his own clumsiness when heading down some stairs. David and Linda, almost certainly not convinced, let the matter slide seeing that it made their guest uncomfortable. The conversation veered away into other menial topics, and serenity was restored.

After the meal was consumed, Chase and David retired to the quiet of the living room while Linda occupied herself in the kitchen. As they entered the room, Chase noticed two certificates hanging on the wall next to a well-stocked and cluttered bookshelf. The first was a Masters Degree in Art from the University of Chicago. The second was a Doctorate in Theology from some Bible school that Chase did not recognize. Regardless, Chase was impressed by the accomplishments, and a growing excitement was rising up in him. *Here was someone worth talking to,* he thought in a rather conceited way. Although Chase would never openly admit it, he had a growing sense of pride in his own intellect. Chase possessed an inner feeling of superiority about people his own age. Even in times of misery and self-loathing, when recognizing his own confusion and anger, he was able to take a twisted sense of pride in his own *recognition* and *consciousness* of his position! It was a comic tragedy—pathetic, timeless, disgusting.

None of this crossed his mind as he sat down opposite his host. Chase's one thought was confrontation. He started in abruptly, not caring to mince words any longer. He wanted the real and raw, and he leapt straight to the heart of the matter.

"I don't want to sound rude or offensive after you've been so hospitable, but I find your faith in God to be somewhat of a stretch. You strike me as an intelligent person, and it would seem your degrees speak on your behalf also—but how? How can you believe in a loving God when you look out at the world around you? How do you *prove* his existence?"

"Chase, I'm not offended in the least. In fact, I find your honesty and straightforwardness refreshing. Let me see how I can explain my own position here for you, you pose an excellent question.

"First, let's spend some time examining what you mean by asking me to *prove* the existence of God. This is important, and I will have to go on to explain what I mean by this and its implications, but there is no way to prove 100% beyond a doubt that God exists. There is simply no way. We as human beings are finite, and we do not possess the necessary faculties and knowledge to prove logically the existence of God. However, the same is true on the other hand as well. No one can prove 100% that God does not exist. This leaves us somewhere in the middle, seeking *proofs* of God's existence, not *proof.* Do you follow me so far?"

"Yeah. So what you're getting at is that, as humans, our reason falls short of comprehending God, which leaves us trying to decide which side of the argument seems to offer the best explanation, Basically, is there more evidence *for* God or *against* Him, right?"

"Yes, for the most part. Now, if you are looking for arguments for God's existence, I will lay out a few that Thomas Aquinas offered hundreds of years ago, and that are still relevant today. Have you ever heard of Thomas Aquinas before?"

"I think I've heard the name, but I've never read any of his works."

"Aquinas was a philosopher, who lived roughly seven hundred and fifty years ago in Italy. He became Catholic later in life, and one of his major pieces of work involved his arguments for the existence of the Transcendent, or God if you prefer. Aquinas advanced five proofs for the existence of God. I'll try to paraphrase as best I can and also give you a quick summary of Aquinas' thought process or worldview.

"Aquinas believed that there were two distinct forms of knowledge: the natural knowledge that we find in philosophy and the supernatural knowledge that is revealed through God and falls into the realm of theology. Natural knowledge is anything we, as humans, can attain through the sciences and our reason apart from any sort of divine revelation. Supernatural knowledge pertains to any knowledge about the character of God. It is knowledge God imparts to us so that we might know and have fellowship with him. It is primarily given to us from the Bible, but we cannot rule out other means that the divine may choose to use—back to the five proofs, though. They are as follows: the argument from motion or change, the argument from cause and effect to a first cause, the argument from contingent beings to a necessary being, the argument from degrees of perfection to a perfect being, and finally one that you might be more familiar with, which is essentially the argument for a creator or designer due to the incredible amount of design we encounter in everything around us and in ourselves.

"Now, the first argument centers on the fact that things move or change. This means that they must first possess the *potential* for change, and according to Aquinas, no potentiality can actualize itself without some prior event influencing a change. This puts us in an infinitely long scenario where one action causes another reaction and so on forever and ever. The problem arises in the fact that there is a need of a Prime Mover, some force that independently instituted all the change and motion outward from itself. It is sort of along the lines of the big bang theory if you will, with the main problem to that theory being how that bang came from nothing and created everything. The second argument of cause and effect hinges along the same principle, so also does the argument for a designer for the design—basically that there has to be a first cause, a starting point, a creator. So we'll now take a look at the third and fourth arguments Aquinas presents.

"When arguing for degrees of perfection, Aquinas explores the idea that in order for us as people to be able to determine that *A* is better than *B*, or that *A* is more beautiful, good, or right than *B;* we must first have an idea as to the standard of beauty, truth, and goodness. You see, we could never know that *B* falls short of the standard, unless there exists some sort of pre-established, perfect standard. And that perfect standard, says Aquinas, is God. Finally, we get into his third proof, and personally, I think his most convincing argument for the existence of the divine: the persuasion toward a necessary being to explain all contingent beings.

"A necessary being is a being whose existence is not dependent on anything outside of itself, and whose nonexistence is impossible. So a necessary being is both eternal and self-sufficient. A contingent being on the other hand is something that is able to be nonexistent, and whose existence depends on some other force outside of itself. We are not self-sufficient. We are not able to give life to ourselves. Neither is any other contingent being, which as far as we can tell, every being that makes up the world and universe and dwells in it is a contingent being. There is no explanation as to why we exist short of some sort of necessary being that supports a contingent universe populated with strictly contingent beings. I know that is a lot to swallow all at once; do you have any questions on anything so far? Feel free to interrupt anytime."

"No, I was able to follow fairly well. Aquinas does provide convincing evidence for the existence of *some* sort of transcendent power. I'm not going to argue that. But just because there may be some external power out there, it doesn't mean that it is the loving, "personal" God like you believe. Looking around, I'd say if there ever was a God who created us, he left us alone a long time ago."

"That is a fair accusation. This world does not seem to reflect a perfect and loving creator does it? There is pain, misery, death, atrocities, and hate. How can people believe, when there appears such an illogical contradiction between what God reveals of Himself in the Bible and what the world radiates? We have to look at three things to understand this seeming contradiction: human free will, the sacrifice Jesus Christ made on the cross, and God's ultimate plan.

"First, let's reconsider that for there to be free will, there has to be, both right and wrong, good and evil. Since it is against the very nature of God to be evil, we realize that evil was not created by God, but it was allowed to *happen*. This is a very important distinction, for if God's only purpose in allowing evil was to cause grief, misery, and condemnation, we would have nothing but a cosmic sadist with us at His mercy. Thankfully, this is not the case. God allowed Satan to tempt mankind in order that they might *choose* to follow Him. However, like I mentioned before in my sermon, man is not faultless, and both male and female succumbed to the temptation. Now, as a result of that sin, all of creation has been tainted, and Satan has had dominion over the world. This does not mean that God is not there, or that He does not care. He cared so much that He put on flesh and died for us—suffering every single sin ever committed or ever to be committed as He died agonizingly on the cross. He did this so that man might have a way back into fellowship with Him. God not only is not the cause of suffering, but He Himself has *felt* every single pain every one of us has ever felt. Can you imagine? Christ is the definition of love—there is nothing more profound than that act of love.

"The idea that God just sits back and does nothing when there are so many problems around might seem plausible, but it is not that He doesn't want to help—He has done everything short of dropping from the sky with a microphone to get our attention. We are not required to *work* our way to heaven, or to be smart enough to get in, or to go to church enough or to even *love* him enough to get in. All he desires is for us to accept his gift. All the murders, lies, rapes, abuses, and pain comes from us trying on our own to live apart from the Giver of life, desperately lost and separated from truth, pursuing the 'shadows on the wall' as Plato would put it. As long as we live, as long as life exists on this planet, there will be pain. We have sinful natures, and until we are raised again in our new bodies we will continue to hurt ourselves and others around us. It is the human tragedy, mournful to both our eyes and God's, but it works out for good nevertheless."

"That's all well and fine, but if there were a God, you would think He would be able to work out a better way of doing things."

"Let me ask you something. When you look around you, at the billions of stars in the night sky, at the diverse and amazing assortment of animals and plants, at the complexity of a single molecule, at the courage, love, caring, and perseverance people are able to exhibit, how does that fit your worldview? Do you not see the beauty?"

"I have seen beauty in life, and have met amazing people, but so what? Are you actually implying I should buy into the idea of God because there are good people and beautiful things in life? I say that that is just humanity shining through, good acts and beautiful creations are just examples of the human spirit triumphing in the dark. There is no reason why God needs be behind good acts."

"From your experiences, Chase, what is the nature of man?"

"Do you mean do I think mankind is basically good or bad? I see humanity as selfish, self-centered—they toil only for themselves. People are like animals fighting to survive. We waste and exhaust the earth's resources, and fight over every piece of land that is useful. Eventually, we will all blow ourselves to hell with bombs and guns and nukes. We see it coming and cannot avoid it. We are a race of gifted savages, and soon we will exist no more. People are too damn self-centered to change a thing."

"That is a rather gloomy outlook, and I would have to agree for the most part. People are selfish, bent toward their own satisfaction, and greedy. They are just like Adam and Eve in the garden. They had everything they could ever need, but they wanted more. Eve wanted to be like God, and Adam wanted Eve for his happiness; that is why they fell."

"I can understand free will and how this is 'the only way' God could have done it or whatever, but how do you explain hell. Anyone who does not believe just like you in your God is going to hell to burn for all eternity. Where is your loving God now?"

"All people will be raised from the dead one day and given eternal bodies to match the eternal soul they already possess. Then Christ, and Christ alone, will judge the hearts of each and every person. Some will pass on into paradise with Him, others will not. This is not because God is unmerciful, for it says in the Bible that 'He is unwilling that any should perish,' but it is because He is a just and holy God. Every single person has the opportunity to know Him. He would not be able to justly condemn them if this opportunity were not afforded. However, it is now, right here on earth, which is God's period of mercy. God could come back anytime he wanted, but he is holding out as long as possible so that as many people as possible will be given a chance to repent. He cannot, and will not, give free passes on the Day of Judgment. This would negate promises He made to us in the Bible, and it would negate His very nature should He break his word."

"It just seems so sadistic to let people burn forever and ever. How can you sleep peacefully at night knowing that millions of people, people you have known, will burn for all eternity? If that's God's justice, I want nothing to do with your God or anything He promises."

"The idea of hell is the toughest thing to deal with in the entire Bible. I struggled a lot with it when I first became a Christian, and you know what? I still cringe. It is immensely terrible to think of. It's a horrible thought that people will be punished forever for the sin in their life. Something you said interests me though, twice you said that people will *burn* in hell. Why?"

"Uh, isn't that what happens in hell? Fire and brimstone and all that? Or am I horribly mistaken or something? Is hell all about dartboards, saunas, and partying with the Prince of Darkness?"

"Not exactly, but the truth of the matter is that we don't know much about heaven or hell. All we have to go off of is the Apostle John's account in the book of Revelation, and his ability to describe accurately what he actually perceived in heaven by human means of understanding is questionable to say the least. How would you describe the things of heaven with earthly words? It is just not reasonable to assume the descriptions we have are completely full. John uses the only thing he can: similes. He described hell, the place of eternal suffering, as being a place of fire and brimstone because that is the best way he has to connote pain. God is infinitely more knowledgeable and righteous than we ever could be, so you can bet that he did a much better job in designing his system of punishment and rewards than any of us could ever do. We will not fully understand it all until we are raised flawless and complete in His image.

"We are incapable of judging the Creator simply because we cannot accurately or fully understand all the intricate workings and conditions in His plan. In all honesty, the only thing we can know for sure is that hell is indeed a place of punishment and heaven is a place of glory. The details are not for us to judge. The real cause of anguish in hell though, apart from anything else that may be going on, is the eternal separation from the love of God. People will realize then that they were given chance after chance after chance, and still they sought after their own desires and scorned their Maker. The realization of this, of their forever lost opportunity at joy—this is their torment. Separation from God is the cause of our misery—this is also true of life on this earth. Disconnection with our Creator is a source of discontent and trouble, but it is a useful trouble! For by it people are led to seek the truth, and by that they are led toward God."

"All right, fair enough. But what if a person finds God in Islam, or Buddhism? What then? Every religion says that they are the "right" one. It would appear that I'm damned no matter which way I believe, because one way or another I'm offending some god."

"That is a great question—let's see what we can come up with. First, let us assume for the sake of argument that we believe in God, because if we don't believe in a god, then every religion in the world is not going to mean a thing to us. So assuming that there is indeed a god up there, we now find that there are multiple conflicting views as to whom that god is, and how one should go about knowing him. Obviously, if there is only one all powerful being, and there are many conflicting groups, then not all can be true, though many may contain fragments of truth.

"I am not going to sit around and tell you that my beliefs are right, and yours along with everyone else's are wrong. I am not one to disparage the beliefs of others just to try and make mine look good. Every religion has things going for them, but as I said before, not every religion can be right. They all possess elements of truth, and everyone has to search for the Creator in the best way they can, with all their heart. I am not going to tell you what to believe. You have to discover that for yourself. If your mind and heart are open, though, you will hear God calling you. We are poor discerners of truth in our own right. God must reveal Himself to us. No amount of seeking or yelling will help you find truth—God will reach out to you if you are looking for Him, and He will do it often when it is least expected."

"Okay...but maybe all religions are wrong in themselves. Like, think about this for a second. I believe religions are the cause of more harm than anything else, look at the inquisition or the crusades for crying out loud! What is that? Every religion is full of liars and hypocrites, people who use religion because it makes them feel better. They use it, but if it's ever an inconvenience they bend the rules. Why is that? Because *they* are the ones who control their god, not the other way around. They bought into it in order to cope with the world, but when the going gets tough, almost none of them would stand firm, because they just don't honestly believe in anything. People are pathetic. Humanity is hideous. All their attempts to hide behind some sort of forgiving God or loving religion are the biggest cop out imaginable … nothing personal, that's just what I see."

"Why do you think that is? How is it that religions or the church have been responsible for so much damage?"

"Because it's a lie! If there was a divine power behind people telling them to kill and rob others, then I for one want no part of whatever that god is offering. The most likely answer is simply that there is not, and never was, a god behind any of it. They created the lie. They fabricated the theory to justify their own horrific deeds."

"It is rather atrocious isn't it? How human's can use anything, even something they claim to revere as sacred, to validate their actions. Do you think though, honestly, that if God really is like what he claims in the scriptures to be, that he actually was behind any of those horrible cruelties done to innocent people?"

"Well, how would you take it? Does hearing about that make you giddy to jump up and pledge allegiance to the church and God?"

"No, no it wouldn't. It would confuse me. It would make me question why a group of people who claim to follow the Bible and all that it says about loving one's neighbor, and giving to the poor, would go out and do almost the exact opposite. Do you think you know how that could happen or why that is Chase?"

"Because people are rotten."

"So optimistically put."

"Call it like you see it, right? That is how I see it."

"Well you are pretty much right. It was never God's order to attack and ransack and kill people in His name, no matter the cause. It was a human affair all the way. Greed motivated some, like those in control and in power, and in other cases, people honestly thought they were doing the right thing. It's tragic, but if the church leaders told you to do something, that it was "God's will," and you were uneducated and, more often than not, forced to go off and fight, you would. Yes, religions and their leaders have been responsible for horrible things, but it is never the will of God for people to commit such acts in His name. Never. Man in his ignorance and sin is always the cause of suffering, not God."

"How … how can you be sure? How can you *know* that any of it is true? When every argument on every side sounds good, how do you know?"

"If you look for absolute assurance in what I have said, I am sorry Chase. There is nothing I, or anyone else, can ever say to convince you or anyone of the truth. No argument, no rhetoric, no logic, no matter how sound, has ever led a single person to truth and to God. They are only words. Only God himself can open a person's eyes to see Him. For is it man who receives the glory for bringing people to salvation and belief in the Transcendent? No, all glory is God's—for it is He who loved us enough to die for us, He who opens our eyes to see His truth, and He who is coming again to redeem us unto Him. He is beyond our own faculties, only implied by the things all around us."

The dialogue between the two ended then in silence. Chase sat not knowing what to say. He sat not knowing what to think. The stillness was broken by Linda's footsteps as she walked into the room.

"I thought you two might like some coffee," she said, smiling. In her hands was a small silver tray with coffee, sugar, and cream resting on its reflective surface. She set the tray down between them and retreated from the room again.

David began reaching for the coffee, but Chase jumped up. David looked at Chase, raising his eyebrows.

"I should get going," Chase blurted out. "I still have to make it past Portland today."

"Do your relatives live out near the beach?" David inquired. "The Pacific Ocean is only about two hours past Portland heading West."

"Uh, they live in between Portland and the beach I guess. I really do need to get going though..."

"No problem, I understand. Listen, Chase, I want you to know that you're welcome here on your way back through if you feel like stopping by. We'd love to see you again. It was good talking with you. You have a sharp mind—a seeking mind. Don't ever feel embarrassed to ask questions and look for the answers. You're a good kid. Take care of yourself out there and remember to stop by on your way back home."

Chase nodded his head, turned his back, and jogged out to his Jeep. His mind was swimming all over the place, and grabbing the steering wheel, he realized he was shaking. He sat still for a moment, trying to organize his thoughts. Finally, he twisted the key, and the car fired to life. Chase backed from the driveway feeling disoriented and lost. He gazed around to find his bearings, and set off toward the gas station. Once there, he filled up his gas tank, and practically jumped across the counter to pick out a pack of cigarettes. Not waiting till he was outside, he lit one up as he walked through the glass doorway.

He was scared and didn't know why.

He lit another cigarette in the parking lot and smoked it before getting back in the Jeep. Sitting behind the wheel, he became anxious to leave. He did not know where he would go. He only knew that he had to get out of this town before he lost it. With the gas pedal to the floor and eyes trying to focus only on the road, Chase peeled out, fleeing toward the edge of the earth.

CHASE

Under the crooked smile of a Cheshire moon, a small pair of phosphorescent lights appeared overlooking the vast, dark blue plain. The pair of lights came to rest alone in the small outlook area, far above the placid ocean surface below. A scattering of speckled stars stained the black sky above. A small shape emerged from where the lights suddenly went out. The figure moved right up to the railing and stood there, pausing, motionless. The figure stood there for a long time with the darkness threatening to swallow it whole and the immensity of everything before its eyes glimpsing it and laughing. The moon knew. It knew, but refused to whisper its secret—choosing instead only silence and a bent smile. Time froze. The muffled sound of waves far below faded. The wind died. The stillness and silence came crushing in.

There, far above the Pacific Ocean, Chase Pollard looked out at a sea and sky looking in on him. In the stillness he felt his limbs trembling. The spinning, grinding, tearing, and filching of time had all stopped. He stood in that frozen moment of nothingness and infinity and let it carry him off.

Absolutes or not? Amidst the wind, above the trees, weaving in a rainbow of living colors both visible and invisible. Is it wrong to be terrified? Or right to feign indifference? Have I plunged through shale only to pause on the periphery?

Either everything matters or nothing does. Which is worse?

I am so sick and tired of being sick and tired. But that's no excuse... I can't compromise over truth. No, never.

I'm scared aren't I? I'm scared nothing has changed. Here I stand... somewhere... and I am still the same. It's like we're all creatures of habit, trapped in glass cages of the familiar. Spinning. Laughing. Drowning.

Maybe it's not that bad.

Depression is familiar. Despair is an old friend— always around, but you get used to them, and in time you would take them over nothing. Who would I be if I wasn't plagued by sleepless nights, drug cravings, and pointless depression? I would not be. It has lived in me so long that the face I try harder and harder to put on every day becomes the lie. That is not me anymore. I do not know what I am, or would be, or can be.

Why am I here?

Is this God's work? Is He here? Is that Him in the wind? There is no wind... but I feel!

No!

We are all alone! I am alone! I am so alone...

It's true isn't it? I am unable to deal... so I am search-ing for meaning in an absurd world. And guess what? There is none! Ha, ha, and that's how it really is. What now then?

I will live on. I can live on however I want. There is no one who can judge me.

Silver coins for the eyes of fate.

The freedom to be the master of one's own destiny! To care not whether one is remembered, forgotten, beautiful, malicious, emetic, or creative! Dust to dust and nothing more. Life is an accident, and I will face the nothingness of death with a cocky smirk.

If I could pick all the dirty flowers in the world, I would make them into something beautiful.

I would survive. I could survive in a world without order or eternal consequences. I would read the poetry off the souls of my muddy shoes and lap ocean spray with an inquisitive tongue. The bark off the trees would be my map and guide. I could slowly kill the screaming voice in my chest, and it would grow smaller and smaller until it finally spoke no more...

"There is a voice though... it's there. I can hear it inside; what about that voice? Maybe there is some-thing else after all..."

"Whoa. Careful with that kind of thinking—what are you doing?"

"I'm just considering the small chance that ... "

"What? No! There is no God up there trying to talk you. Are you insane? Look at you! You are alone—and you have to deal with that."

"But why am I here? Was I led out here by something?"

"Yeah, something that is telling you to jump. And you know why? Because it hates you. God hates you."

"No ... it's not true ... "

"It is. Do you really believe that after all you've been through, the drunkenness, the drugs, the hatred—it was because something somewhere out there likes you? There is nothing out there, and if there is, you ought to be screaming at it instead of trying to befriend it. That is the sad truth of it. Look at you! Get hold of yourself—it's not so terrible. You are free! You can do anything your heart desires! Every pleasure is open to you!"

"You hate me."

"What? Don't be stupid."

"You are trying to destroy me."

"Is there really no talking to you right now? Whatever. It doesn't matter. Within a few days, you'll be back to staring down at the bottom of a bottle. You can't create happiness, and you sure can't find any."

"You may be right."

"Yes."

"I probably am incapable of creating any kind of happiness for myself. I probably can't change my habits over-

I TOSS TILL DAWN

night. I probably can't live a perfect little life either... but it doesn't matter what I do, or can't do. God is greater than I am, and He can help me."

"Sure, maybe God can help you... but why would He? What are you to Him? He hasn't cared about you up till now—why should He now?"

"You're wrong. God would not create people without having a plan for each one of them. God loves everyone... even me."

"No! No! You're wrong! God can't love you! You're a pervert, a liar, and a blasphemer! You're not good enough!"

"Yes, it's true. I am not good enough, but neither is anyone else. I am not worthy, but I can be forgiven."

"No! You've cursed God in your words and with your heart! There is no hope for you!"

"No. You're wrong. Everything I have ever done, or will ever do—from the vilest act, to smallest—God will forgive. All I have to do is ask."

"No!"

"Leave me! Get out, and don't come back! I won't let you to destroy me any longer! I am free and perfect in God's sight... and He loves me."

The world came into focus. It came into true focus for the first time in Chase's life. Nothing around him had changed, but it all had become different. Chase had to sit down; it was all too much to take in. His heart

191

was on fire, and tears of joy streamed freely down his cheeks. He stared up at the night sky with a trembling smile on his face. For the first time in his life, his mind and heart were open. Oh the joy that leapt in his soul! It was impalpable, imperishable. He felt the earth unraveling before him. This was not an end to freedom or expression or individuality—it was the start of it. Through failures, and triumphs, and obstacles, and trials he would never again be alone. This was not the establishment of a new purpose or meaning; it was the embrace of the one that had always been there.

Chase raised his eyes to the heavens, saying the only thing he could think to utter in the midst of his awe:

"Thank you ... thank you ... thank you ..."

Chase stood still for a long time and just listened to the beat of his heart. A cool, salty breeze caressed his body. He breathed deeply.

Chase turned and got in his car then. He started the engine and slowly backed out of his parking spot. Turning toward home, he drove off into the night. In his mind he saw Miriam's face smiling back at him.

A grin crept onto his face.

"I'm coming, Miriam," he said aloud. "I'm all right ... and I'm coming back to you."

The moon beamed down from above, and Chase, staring up into the night sky, understood why the moon smiled.